LIFE RAFT

stories by Ken Nash

Published by Equus Press
Copyright © 2019 by Ken Nash
Cover and design by Ken Nash
Composed in Sabon, designed by Jan Tschihold (1967)

The publisher wishes to acknowledge the generous support of James H. Ottaway, Jr.

Printed on acid-free paper

ISBN 978-0-9931955-9-4 (pbk)

About *Life Raft*

"Ken Nash is not like the rest of us. Not only does he actually listen to what people say and how they say it, he can reproduce it expertly. In his endlessly inventive stories, Freud's concept of the uncanny (*unheimlich*) applies — these eerie slices of alternate reality, set in garbage dumps and dystopian future societies, look and feel just a little too much like where we're headed. But not only can he see into the future, he can make us laugh through our fright. There is mordant wit; there is trenchant social observation. If Ken Nash didn't exist, we would have to invent him. But we can't. Because inventing Ken Nash is a job for one person only: Ken Nash. We're lucky we get to enter his weird and deeply affecting worlds."

— Donna Stonecipher, author of *Transaction Histories*

"In Ken Nash's brilliant and delightful new story collection, the world does not merely stand on end, it tumbles over again and again. Here is a world that is at once familiar and recognizable, and yet also strange and bizarre enough for the unexpected and magical to happen. A master of the casually surreal encounter (wherein the very weird is presented as the most normal thing in the world), Nash's stories brim with wit and charm. His warm and effortlessly humorous prose recalls Calvino and Atwood — writers whose keen eyes for social foibles expose not just the world we live in, but the world we are sleepwalking ever closer to. In each of these brief vignettes, Nash skewers reality – and the myths we use to console ourselves – with the precision of a well-aimed dagger."

— Joshua Mensch, author of *Because: A Lyric Memoir*

"In these deft, quirky, darkly hilarious stories, the mundane realities of vacations, conferences, and dive bars, of delayed flights and broken furnaces, are intruded on at every turn by the surreal and absurd. Ken Nash's narrators wander and wonder, befuddled but hopeful observers of secret worlds whose rituals they're not entirely privy to, worlds in which nothing can be taken for granted.

An aspiring milliner goes to visit a five-headed demon, with unexpected results; a rebellious artist whose medium is the weather runs afoul of the authorities; a man may or may not have encountered his own reincarnated self.

In exuberant, precise prose suffused with dream logic and brilliant, luminous flashes of wonder, these stories revel in the sinister and delightful, taking the reader to a place not easily forgotten."

— Holly Tavel, author of *The Weather in Fritz Bemelmans Park*

Previous praise for Ken Nash's *The Brain Harvest*

"*The Brain Harvest* is an eclectic, deceptively witty collection of short fiction that represents the crystallisation of one of Prague's most resourceful and imaginative English-language writers."

— Stephan Delbos, *The Prague Post*

"Nash has the ability to put the reader into a story with the first paragraph and keeps hold of you until the end."

— Joe Sherman, author of *In the Rings of Saturn*

"*The Brain Harvest* by Ken Nash taught me: precision and compression and crazy hope, how if we zoom in far enough in anyone's life, the absurdities reveal a depth of honesty and wonder."

— Ryan Werner, *Necessary Fiction*

"The stories in Ken Nash's brilliant collection *The Brain Harvest* lay bare the sparks and idiosyncrasies of an exceptional mind. Each new story is distinct and memorable in its jewel-like compactness, and the characters we meet are unique and endearing. In subject matter, the stories weave and delve into continuously unexpected territory; from the alien adventures of Emily Dickinson, to the intricacies of bespoke basket-making, time travel, orchestral garden plots, and the great green sea lizards that haunt our parents' dreams. Nash's playful and quick-witted style bears echoes of maverick American greats like George Saunders and Donald Barthelme, and recalls the quirkiness of Miranda July. Taut, intelligent, eccentric, and wholly engaging, *The Brain Harvest* is a wonderful debut for a very talented new writer."

— Clare Wigfall, author of *The Loudest Sound and Nothing*

CONTENTS

The Passenger

Not long before my death, I stumbled upon an old tattered paperback left behind at the Wood Beach Shelter. It was missing a back cover and there were water stains along the fore-edge from having been left in the rain. It was written by a former Buddhist monk and it explained the concept of life and reincarnation. According to the author, people rarely returned as human beings. Life exists in many forms and people are only a small and not wholly significant portion of all our earthly abundance.

I kept the book on the truck seat next to me as I drove from town to town searching for items to salvage from dumpsters and along residential streets before the trash collectors came. I worked early mornings, starting before sunrise. I'd keep at it until I'd collected and sold enough salvage to cover my expenses for a day or two.

On a good day I'd earn enough for a Denny's Grand Slam, two bottles of Old Heaven Hill, a pack of Winston's and an eight-dollar room at Motel 6. On a bad day I might make it to a soup kitchen, maybe microwave a burrito at 7-11 and, likely, surreptitiously acquire a flask of Night Train or bottle of Boons. I'd drink in the truck while parked in some distant lot behind a shopping mall or warehouse. Then I'd crawl beneath newspaper circulars in the back seat and sleep.

The old Monk's book was not something I ever read cover to missing back cover. I would pick it up and read whatever the pages opened to.

> *The will to life is a stream from the east flowing toward the west following the direction of the sun...*

> *...alone we are one drop of rain; together we are one ocean...*

> *That which is ONE in spite of being the many, that alone we call the Mystery...*

Many times I told myself, *Enough of this shit.* I threw the book out the window on several occasions, but each time I eventually turned the truck around, drove back and searched along the side of the road within the tall grass, briar and thicket to retrieve the damn thing.

In Brownsville, I salvaged a Kenmore refrigerator in good working order, some brass table lamps and a box of porcelain fixtures. I celebrated that afternoon at a dive called The Wagon Wheel. That's where I met Clark, this young tattooed guy headed to Philly to visit his girlfriend, or ex-girlfriend, and their kid.

"People are shit," he said. "Take me. There is nothing you can point to and say, *Now there's something you've done, Clark, that's made the world a better place.* All I've ever done is burn through God's creation, taken whatever I've needed to survive and left nothing but a trail of misery and piss in my wake."

"You have a son, though, Clark. That's *something.* You've reproduced. Is there anything more fundamental than that?"

"Shit. I just created another *me* that's gonna chew away at whatever's left of this world when I'm done. Don't get me wrong. I love the little shit. That's why I'm desperate to get back and see him, let him know he's still got a pop. But let's be realistic. I'm not doing the world any service creating another life that's just gonna continue on with *this.*" He gestured toward the bar and its patrons. "*This,*" he said again.

Clark and I drank Rolling Rock and bourbon shots all afternoon, until the bartender started avoiding eye contact and staying away from our end of the counter. Just as well. A few more drinks and my morning's work would be all for nought. I'd be sleeping in the truck again, instead of beneath a warm, comfy quilt at the Route 9 Motel 6.

"Mind giving me a lift?" Clark asked, as we toppled off our barstools to leave.

"How'd you get here in the first place?"

"Walked from Station Drive. Got dropped off there by my last ride."

"You hitchin' all the way to Philly?"

"That's right."

We drove to the 7-11, got a bottle of Crow and killed it off at the Motel 6.

The next morning I was seriously wrecked. I didn't want to get out of bed. Couldn't bear the thought of trawling the town for salvageables. But Clark was a fuckin' machine.

"Get a move on, buddy," he said, with a kick to the box spring. "Beautiful day out there. Let's go get ourselves some pancakes."

"Fuck off," I grumbled. He pulled open the curtains. The sun bore down like a hot iron pressed to my skull. "Rise and shine, you stinky old possum."

When we walked outside there was only an old Nike shoe box where the truck had been parked.

"Where's my truck?!"

"What truck?"

"My truck! The one I parked here last night."

"Dude, we walked the entire way. If you had a truck, it's back at the bar."

"Are you fucking kidding me?"

"You think either of us could have driven last night? You were barely walkable."

I kicked the shoebox and it went tumbling across the pavement, lid flying off.

"It's not the box's fault, dude. Let's get some pancakes."

"I'm getting the truck first."

At the I-HOP, Clark flipped through my book while drinking his third coffee refill. He read out loud, "'Those who are pure and seek to attain each stage of progress are called Arhats. The Arhat is able to fly through space and assume different forms; his life is eternal and there are times when he causes heaven and earth to quake.' *Those who are pure.* What do you think he means by *pure?*"

I mopped up residual syrup with some toast. I was hungrier than I'd thought. It had taken a while to finally get to Denny's. Someone had smashed the passenger window on the truck. We had to clean out glass particles and find some plastic sheet to tape over the missing window. Nothing was stolen. Whoever it was, though, left behind a damp and dirty toy monkey, the sort you might win at a carnival shooting gallery, were you able to shoot straight with one of those bent-up pellet guns.

"Nothing is pure," Clark said, answering his own question.

"That's right. Nothing. Nothing and everything."

"Dude, you sound like a philosopher."

"Shit. I'm just tired and pissed off. Are you finished with that coffee? I got things to do."

"I'm sure you do." He closed the book, emptied the mug into his face, and set the empty cup on a napkin sopped in coffee rings. "Shall we skedaddle?"

We drove toward Summerfield with the toy monkey on the seat between us. I told Clark I would take him as far as Greenwood. In exchange, he would help with some hauling and throw in some gas money. We didn't talk most of the way. The plastic taped over the passenger window shuddered loudly and convulsed like a bag full of bats flapping their wings. It made me uneasy the way Clark kept prying into my book. I wanted to grab it away. Instead, I focused on my breathing, the stream of air flowing from nostrils to hairs on my upper lip.

"*The journey is a thousandfold,*" said Clark, his voice raised to nearly a shout, trying to overcome the whip and thwack of rustling plastic. "*The destination is only this one moment.*"

"What's that?" I said, barely able to discern his words. "The reservation is for strangers?"

"Partners," said Clark and grinned.

"What about partners?"

"There are clouds that share similar names."

"I have no idea what you're talking about, guy."

We entered Summerfield and stopped at the first filling station. I poured leaded into the tank, while Clark did some exercise stretches in the parking lot. When finished stretching, Clark went inside to pay. I opened the truck door, grabbed the book and shoved it deep beneath the driver seat.

We drove to a field I knew where people liked to abandon old furniture, appliances and worthless car bodies. After a mile or so, Clark began patting the seat and rummaging around.

"Where's that book?" he said.

"I put it away."

He opened a beer and drank from the can. We drove on in silence until the road turned to gravel, then dirt. We were out in some field I hadn't recognized. I thought maybe I'd gone the wrong way.

"What kind of trees are those?"

"Peach," I said. They were blooming early. An Easter freeze would likely kill off the flowers or keep them from setting fruit this year.

As the road began to bang us around a bit, I slowed the truck.

"This is how I picture Heaven," Clark said.

"You believe in that?"

"Not saying I do, not saying I don't. I suppose anything's possible. Maybe even what it says in that book about reincarnation. I could come back as something better."

"Or something worse."

"Ya. I suppose with my karma I'm not coming back as the King of Siam. What do you think you'd be in the next life?"

"A tire iron."

"Fuck me. Why a tire iron?"

"A tire iron gets to go places, can be useful in an emergency and doesn't have a care in the world."

"That sounds like you already."

"Shit. I've nothing to aspire to then."

We drove past the orchard and spotted a trail of black smoke rising in the distance. I figured that's where the dump was, so we headed in that direction. A haze of dust spread behind us, as we moved through the tall grass and thistle. When we came to some railroad tracks, I stopped the truck to look around.

"Drive over it," Clark said.

"I ain't getting run over by a train."

"There's no train coming."

"What if we get stuck on the tracks."

"You ain't getting stuck on those tracks. And if you do, I'll push us off."

I don't know what made me listen to a fool like Clark, but I slowly drove onto the tracks. The front wheels got over the first rails fine, but then stuck in the gravel. They spun in place, kicking rock and sand against the chassis. I rolled down my window and Clark got out. He walked to the rear and started pushing. In the distance, a train whistle began barking like an angry hound.

I worked the pedal and shift. We rocked the truck back and forth against the rails. "Slowly," he yelled. I popped open my door in case I needed to make a jump for it. But the wheels soon caught and the tires rose over the second set of rails. The truck cleared the tracks before the train even came into view.

Clark hopped back into the passenger seat. "Thought we were going to need a tire iron there for a second." He opened another beer.

Sweat was dripping down my face and neck. "Give me one of those," I said.

The dump smelled of burning plastic. Someone had set a motorized wheelchair on fire, its foam cushions smouldering black clouds, its plastic components sagging as they melted into a sad heap of plastic, rubber and wire.

"What the fuck," said Clark. "Someone must have just been here."

The chair was not the only thing burning. There was an old mattress and a pile of magazines billowing flame and smoke.

"Some juvenile arsonist getting off. Must have run when he saw us coming."

The stench was filthy. I pulled my t-shirt up over my nostrils. There were a few good items I knew could sell in town. They'd be easy enough to load into the truck. A Maytag washer. A Whirlpool range. A wooden bed frame with headboard. The Cutlass Supreme with smashed windows would need a bit of dismantling, but seemed promising for parts. I got the tool box out of the backseat and set to work, while Clark tried to douse the burning pile of magazines with damp grass clippings and leaves.

"Some of these are *Penthouse* and *Barely Legal*," said Clark, as he kicked through the smouldering wreckage. "*Swank*! Haven't seen one of those since high school."

"Enjoy," I said, as I unlatched the toolbox and, like a surgeon, examined my instruments.

Apart from the smashed front window, the only things missing from the Cutlass were front tires. I popped the hood. Everything looked fine. Probably some kids had taken her for a joy ride and abandoned her here. If the battery wasn't dead, I might be able to hot wire her started. But then what? I wasn't stupid enough to try and sell a stolen car.

It was a chore getting at the ignition wires. They're not accessible from the steering column on a Cutlass and I had to dismantle the dash to get at them. After connecting them, the engine still failed to start.

"Clark, do me a favor. Drive the truck over here. I'm gonna try and jump this thing."

"You going to drive that wreck? Thing only has two wheels, ya know."

"I can fuckin' see that. Just wanna see what else works here."

Clark drove up and popped the hood. When he jumped out of the truck, he was holding the book in one hand and a beer in another.

"Found it," he said.

"Get me one of those," I said.

"Help yourself."

We sat in the truck and watched the evening light pile down upon the tops of the distant peach trees. The sky got pinker and brighter before turning into a dark bruise on the horizon. I wasn't getting to any reclamations centers today. I wasn't going to be sleeping in a nice hotel bed beneath blankets and clean sheets, either.

Clark handed me another beer. It was warm. I began wishing I were anywhere else but out in an open dump in the middle of nowhere.

"Do you think *déjà vu* has to do with past lives?" Clark said, breaking the moment of silence and derailing my train of thought.

"Why? You *déjà vu*-ing?"

"The thought just occurred to me."

"I sure hope not. Would hate to think I'm repeating my life in the same way every single goddamn time. I figure it's some trick the brain plays on ya, like seeing something out the corner of your eye that's not really there. Or hearing voices when there's no one around."

"You sometimes hear voices in your head? That's serious shit. You ought to talk to someone."

"You telling me you never mistook something that wasn't there?"

"Nah. But kind of the opposite."

"How's that?"

Clark spoke about a time living in Philly with his girl. He woke one morning and saw there were muddy footprints in the room. Someone had crept in at night, stood beside their bed, then took off without them knowing.

"I ran through the apartment to make sure nothing was missing. It's such a sick feeling to know you're lying asleep, completely unarmed and vulnerable, and someone can sneak up on you like that.

"So I'm running around swearing up a storm, wanting to kill this creep that's invaded my home. And my girl is, like, 'Clark, stop being so fucking psycho. There's nobody in the apartment. There is no crook. Look at your fucking boots by the door. They're covered with mud. Those are *your own* footprints.'"

"I suppose that's *not seeing* something that wasn't ever there. Not sure that's opposite of what I was thinking."

"But it was there. Only the *nothing* was me."

"I call that a blackout, Clark. That ain't so unusual."

I lay in the front seat of the Cutlass, while Clark stayed awake drinking. I didn't fall asleep right off. I was wishing we'd brought more booze. I tossed and turned on the cracked vinyl. My eyes were shut, but bothered by some floating lights inside my eyelids. I could not get them to go away. Eventually the lights transformed into a memory so old it felt like it came from another lifetime.

It was the summer Danielle and I had been living in New Mexico on what was called a farm, but wasn't actually a farm any more. Just a big garden surrounded by desert. A lot of kids were living there. The main house was full of them. Danielle and I slept in a green canvas tent, which was fine for us. We wanted our privacy. And, frankly, most of those kids were pretty annoying. They were doing psychedelics and talking about whether time was a real thing or even if the world, as we perceive it, was a real thing, and shit like that they'd learned in some college dormitory. As if any of that mattered.

That part of New Mexico was beautiful. I'd never seen a night sky so full of stars. They weren't just pin pricks of light; they formed thick, luminous swarms. Some stars were so bright, they seemed really close, like you could get in a car and, if you drove fast enough, you could reach them by morning.

I felt responsible for Danielle. She could have stayed with her parents, gone to college. Lived a good, normal life. Found a reliable, handsome, young husband. Took a home in the suburbs. But she chose me. *Why?* I asked her. She smiled and, though it was night, I clearly saw every starlit, orange freckle on her beautiful face. She raised her head towards the night sky, brimming with light, and said, "Because of all this!"

One night, I felt sure there'd been someone standing outside our tent. I saw the outline of his shadow. I leapt through the flaps, but he was already gone. Footprints ran off into the desert. I ran after him as fast as I could.

I thought I saw him running up ahead, but wasn't sure. I kept going, waiting for him to tire or to turn around, hoping to catch him heading back toward the farm. But somehow he got away. When I returned to the tent, Danielle was sitting on the ground, wrapped in a wool blanket.

"What?" I said. I tried putting an arm around her. She pulled away.

"You're all wet," she said. I was drenched in sweat.

"Why are you crying?"

"What is it you keep thinking you see?" she said, a mixture of anger and sadness in her voice. She turned her head away. I stared into the campfire. Sparks leapt from its flames and floated into the sky. I could not answer her.

I woke believing I was somewhere else. I became all confused. I had been sleeping and wasn't sure if this was part of the same dream. Or some other dream. Or no dream at all. Out the truck window, a trail of thick smoke poured into the night sky, masking the stars directly above.

I got out of the Cutlass and walked toward the fire. Clark was there, sitting on a couple of old tires he'd pulled from a rubbish heap. He was staring into the flames and drinking from a bottle of Heaven Hill.

"Hey, is that mine?" I said. "Where'd you get that?"

He'd been so deep in thought he hadn't heard me approach. I took the bottle from his hand and gave a chug.

"Bought it at the gas station. Stuck it 'neath the seat. Been savin' it for later."

"You're a sneak is what you are," I said. I took one more swallow and handed it back. In a few moments, the sadness and shock I'd felt over Danielle appearing in the dream dissolved into a warmth in my chest and belly. I sat on the ground, my bootsoles close to the embers.

"Listen," said Clark. "I have a confession to make."

This, I began to think, is where he tells me there is no girlfriend in Philly, no kid waiting for him, that he's on the run from the law, or something of that sort.

"We didn't meet by chance," he said. "I'd been following you, sort of. Don't worry. It's not what you might think."

"What the hell for?"

"There's been some sort of mistake. I wasn't quite sure what it was, but then I started reading that book of yours and it began to make sense."

"I'm not sure anything in that book makes sense."

"Ya. Maybe," said Clark. "But it makes more sense than all the other things that don't make sense." He took another long swig. "Back in Stevens Point, I was in that liquor store when you came in. Thought I recognized you, but couldn't figure out from where. I followed you out to the parking lot. Saw you drive off. In the morning, you passed by while I was hitching. When I got to Brownsville, there you were again."

"The world is full of coincidences. Believe me."

"Thing is, it wasn't a coincidence. I've been sitting here thinking about it and it starts to fit together."

"Are you stoned, Clark?"

"Man, it's not like that. Look at me."

"Yeah? So what?"

"Can you even describe me?"

The flames from the fire flickered and climbed. They cast light upon all the trash and garbage, the old tires, and the strewn bits of magazine, newspaper and plastic bags. It was hard, though, to actually make out his face in this light. I tried to focus, but it kept blurring. Maybe it was the drink. I couldn't make him out or quite recall from memory how he looked.

"You can't see me," he said, "just like you can't see your own self. Get it? I'm you, reincarnated, but all out of sequence. Like I got here before you were finished. I wasn't supposed to be here yet. Don't look at me that way. You know it's true. All that goddamn, fucked up karma. She's the one who should've survived, not you, you old drunk."

"Don't fuck with me, man. It's late and I'm in no mood for this shit."

"It was your idea to drive the truck over the tracks. She said not to. Do you remember? She begged you to listen."

"I swear I will smash your skull if you keep talking, Clark."

Clark took another swig. He stared into the fire and shook his head. "If I have to, I can prove it."

Clark couldn't prove anything other than a knife pressed against someone's neck can get a person to hand over their wallet and keys.

"I'm doing you a favor leaving this here for you," hollered Clark, throwing the old paperback out the passenger-side window. Then he started the truck's ignition.

"You could at least leave me the rest of that bottle," I said, raising myself off the ground.

The bottle came flying out the window and rolled to my feet. Empty.

"Thanks."

Dirt spit from beneath the tires as he tore off. I listened to the wheels crunch sand and gravel until it was out of hearing. Then it was only me standing there, alone, with the smouldering ashes and a cloud of smoke that had grown weary, spreading out like a grimy mist in the early light of dawn.

I picked up the old book, which was now heavily creased on the spine and missing a few pages short from the end. This thing is like a curse, I thought. I should burn it while the embers are still warm. I carried it over to the trash pile and stood staring into the smouldering porn magazines, branches and cardboard.

I should have been furious, but wasn't. To tell the truth, I felt I'd made a narrow escape and was finally free of a dreadful fate. If there's any sort of reincarnation, I'm guessing it's no circle. Nothing sequential. More like a friggin' hall of mirrors, repeating itself like a reflection over and over, one life buried within the next.

Maybe I can only see that now, thanks to Clark. It would be him this time that takes the truck into the desert. *His* girl in the passenger seat. *His* unborn child in her belly. "Stop, Clark!" she'd insist, "Pull over. You're driving too fast." He wouldn't listen, of course, big manly man that he is. "I know every inch of this road," he'd shout back. "I could drive it blindfold."

I dropped the book into the embers. It sent black ash afloat as it landed. I felt both a sense of dread and relief, like flying, the fear and exhilaration of being airborne. *All I ever wanted to be was free*, I had once told Danielle. And yet everything I'd ever done brought me the opposite. I'd begun to believe freedom wasn't even a thing.

I pulled an old Phoenix Cobras baseball cap out of the trash heap and lengthened the plastic strap. The rising sun was too low for the visor to fully shade my eyes. I took one last look around before leaving. I headed back over the railroad tracks and walked along the dirt path from the direction we'd come.

By the time I reached the peach trees, the sun had properly risen. Perspiration dampened my grease-stained shirt, making it cling tight to my back. I tramped along amongst the joyful trees, their upraised arms, balancing trembling pink buds of recurring youth. *Hello*, they greeted me in passing. *Nice to see you again.* A strangely, familiar welcome.

The Good Couple

We are aware the ugly sounds coming from us may be overheard by the good couple next door. There is nothing we can do about it. Except move. And we're not moving. Good couples are everywhere. We would inevitably end up neighbors to yet another good couple. And continue to make our ugly sounds, embarrassing both ourselves and the good couple next door.

We're not bad on our own, only as a couple. At least that's what we tell ourselves, though it's hard to recall a time before we were a couple. There is a certain comfort knowing our ugliness is mutual, a thing we bring out in each other, not something innate in our personal temperaments.

We have never been invited to our neighbors' for drinks. Never asked to sign for packages or sweetheart bouquets. Never petitioned. Never called upon to water houseplants or pressured into multi-level marketing schemes. The sort of things most neighbors do. With the good couple, we have never exchanged more than passing salutations. *Hello...How's it going...Have a good one...Cheerio...*

No, we are not obsessed with the good couple next door, even though we've discovered so much to laud in their style and habits. We've heard them play Nick Drake, Sandy Denny and Alice Coltrane through the walls. They keep the volume low. Nothing there is ever too loud. We hold an ear against the wall to hear anything at all, really. Sometimes an empty glass helps amplify sound. Hold the open end against the wall and press an ear to the bottom. That's how we know they walk barefoot on hardwood floors and sweep with soft-bristle brooms. Their iron skillets are gently stirred over gas flames. Dinners never microwaved, the way we do. Showers last a good 15 minutes, baths even longer. They towel dry, not blow dry, their moist hairless bodies. They make love from behind on a firm, coil mattress — her gasps and squeals stifled, we assume, within silk pillowcases and plush, down comforters.

Sometimes even the absence of sound speaks volumes.

We do not spend an inordinate amount of time thinking about the good couple. We are not like that. We are too absorbed in our own dramas, which involve a lot of smashing tableware, rearranging furniture, shredding shirts, torching documents, free association, pantomime and role play. Bad role play. The worst kind. Shameful, really. I don't even want to go into it other than say there are costumes and phoney accents involved.

Our shouting is mostly inarticulate — *howls from the wilderness of our lost souls!* Our cries escalate, one atop another, never quite forming intelligible language.

We cannot stop. We force the nonsensical out of each other's throats, like sputum from the spit valve of a sousaphone.

You might think alcohol is somehow involved. Or weed. Or prosthetic limbs. And you would not be entirely wrong. Lines get blurred. Barriers wear thin as damp cocktail napkins. Emotions become abraded by Screwdrivers, Whiskey Sours, Tequila Slammers, Velvet Hammers, Purple Hooters, Widow's Kisses. Something inevitably bleeds through, like self-esteem, pride, memory, regret or loss. Alcohol is all we have to lubricate our pain. Smashed bottles are easier to sweep aside than broken dreams.

We are a mess, plainly. So unlike the good couple next door. What do they know about eczema, ulcers, nosebleed and panic attacks? Let them splaterlessly ooze batter into their waffle griddle and half-slice fresh berries into their mimosas. We will be here rubbing coffee grounds into the rayon carpeting; stuffing charred meats into the garbage disposal; tossing soiled blouses and slacks off the fire escape; biting shoulder blades; pulling hair, beards, nipples and toes; ejaculating semen, spit, urine, lubricants and mouthwash every which way.

One day there was a noticeable silence from next door. It was like a silence ensconced in a quiet, wrapped in a hush, embedded in a void and smothered beneath a cold, wet mattress of indifference.

Come here.

Fuck you. You come here.

No, listen. Next door. Come closer.

We passed the listening glass back and forth. It was the only unsmashed remnant of glassware we still possessed.

It was quieter than empty. Too quiet for them to not be home or asleep. We speculated they were dead. Killed by an intruder or asphyxiated by their professional series Thermador gas range. It hadn't occurred to us the good couple next door simply moved away and what we heard was the hollow of empty space, an apartment denuded of furniture, plants, throw rugs, macrame wall hangings and window shades.

A van came for their things mid-day. They were packed and gone in less than an hour. So said Daryl, the man in room 205 who fixes our broken furniture, repairs the holes in the plaster and sets the doors back on their hinges.

Did you know them? we asked.

Sure, a bit. The fella was European, I think. Had an accent. They sometimes moved about at night. Sock-footed. They'd slide themselves across the floor. A swishing noise, you see. And deep breathing. Dancing is my guess. After, they'd turn on the tap. Fill the tub. Soak and splash themselves. Then fry up some bacon. That's what it sounded like, anyway. But I have to admit, I was often too lazy to get up on the ladder and listen properly.

You might think that's where this story ends, if you were the sort of person who did not understand story endings. But there was more. We're skipping ahead in time, a few years later. We were heading home from couples' therapy, freshly enraged with one another. You wouldn't believe the things confessed! The private matters brought to light! The insults and humiliations! The voice mimicry! But let's not get into that now.

We ran into Jack's Pantry for bottles of vodka and some cartons of Tropicana Homestyle. There was a man in the chip aisle wearing a tan overcoat. He watched us while we argued about what's real vodka and what's complete shit. After we paid the cashier, the man in the overcoat blocked our exit. *Hey,* he said. *Hey.* He stood there waiting for us to say something in response, but we were not sure what to say. Finally, he said, *I used to live next door. It was a few years ago. We were neighbors.*

It took a moment to process what he was saying. He did not look like the neighbor we knew, not that we ever had a good look at him. I recall nice teeth, shiny shoes, combed hair. That's nearly it. This man wore a stained overcoat and wrinkled slacks. Dark hairs protruded from his nostrils and the sides of his neck. His teeth were yellow. His eyes pink as crab legs.

That's right, we said. *How's it going?*

You ruined my marriage, he replied. Then smiled to show he was joking. But we did not smile back.

I have to confess, he continued, *we used to hear a lot through those paper-thin walls. Not that we were spying or anything. It was hard not to hear things.*

That's right, we nodded, but kept mute, waiting to hear where this was going.

You were loud. Kept us up some nights. No need to apologize. That's all history. She left. Said we would never have what you have. Crazy, right? I'm not judging. Whatever you're doing works, apparently. Then he started to sob. Right there by the news rack with all those celebrity magazines covers mawkishly grinning.

We took him home with us. What else were we to do? His name, we finally learned, was Ansgar. *What kind of a name is that? Nordic,* he replied. We poured him screwdrivers, fed him Double Stuff Oreos and listened to him talk about Kinsley, his ex-wife who left him to travel through India and connect with her past self. *Selves,* he corrected himself. *She sends postcards, writing of her discoveries. She was once a Vedic priestess praying over fish in the Ganges. Her fingers mysteriously blistered while recalling her time working as a weaver in Anhara.* Ansgar could recount nearly every postcard. She had been a nursemaid for *Pen-the-silea,* Queen of the Amazons. She had been a female pirate in the Guangdong province of China in the 17th century. She wrote sonnets under a male moniker in the late 1800s. She wore a pith helmet in the Carpathian Mountains during World War 1.

I got out the emergency Old Crow from beneath the bathroom sink. We wrapped ice in a towel, and pounded it with a hammer, then tossed the chips into plastic 7-11 mugs along with healthy pours of bourbon. We'd been hiding weed from each other, but we fished out our hidden reserves and rolled one spliff after another. Ansgar held not one objection. He let us pour drinks, light smokes, feed him nacho chips, cheddar cheese popcorn and microwave pork chops.

Ansgar attacked the pork chops as if he hadn't eaten in days. *This is delicious,* he said, even though we knew it wasn't. It had freezer burn and it had been a cheap

cut we bought from the Armenian guy at the farmer's
market before he was deported.

Wonderful, he said, licking the grease from his fingers. *I haven't eaten this well in god knows how long.*
He confessed to falling on hard times after Kinsley left.
He'd been a project manager for a software startup.
Was riding high. Called himself a Scrum master, whatever that is. But their app went crap, and the CFO blew
their IPO when all the Angles fled the incubator. Crazy
talk, I know.

Have some more of these, we said, scooping blackies and yellowies into his palm. *Wash them down with
this,* we said, handing him a mug of absinthe topped
with whipped cream. His nerves began to steady as his
speech began to slur. We felt proud. It was like nursing
the child we swore we would never have.

Ansgar stayed with us a week. He slept on the pullout sofa. We fed him oatmeal with laxatives for breakfast, French fries and Whip-its for lunch. We taught
him how to apply for Food Stamps, where to get pain
medication without a prescription, and ways to procure snacks and toiletries at CVS without getting
caught on their security cameras.

I don't know how to thank you, he said.

Stop! we told him. *Just stop. Have you learned
nothing from us?*

At the end of the week, we told him, *We think
you're ready, Ansgar.* We thought for a moment he
might cry. But he quickly regained composure, rubbing his purplish eyes and alighting a huge smile. He
knew it was the right thing. The time had come for
Ansgar to move on and for us to get back to our ar-

guing, hectoring, plate smashing and brutal, ritualistic love making.

We filled Ansgar's pockets with rolling papers, furniture wax, antihistamines and No Doz tablets. He embraced us both before setting foot out the door. We watched him walk down the long corridor to the stairwell. He was going to be okay, we assured ourselves. Wounds heal all time. A lost child gathers no dust. Even needles have eyes. We walked back inside, slammed the door and began finding fault with each other once more.

The Furnace

I've gone down to check one more time. In a few days it will be removed and replaced with the new one. It's been in our home for nearly twenty-five years. It was here when the twins were born and here when they went off to college. It was here when my husband I separated and here when we reconciled and started again. Everything that's gone on in this house, every noise made, every door slammed or plate broken, every word whispered or spoken, has clattered down these shafts and into its flames. When the furnace makes sounds, when it creaks and pops and rattles and roars, I hardly understand what any of it means, but it feels like some sort of response to everywhere above.

Light from the ceiling bulb barely illuminates the back corner where the furnace stands. I shine the Eveready to see better. I notice nothing problematic, though the furnace repairman says there is a faulty flame sensor, a cracked heat exchanger and a burner orifice that's sized too large. Among other things. He sealed a small leak and replaced the thermocoupler, but didn't think it worth replacing anything else. We needed a new one, he said. A new one, he claimed, would heat more efficiently. With the savings on gas, a new furnace would pay for itself in four or five years. He handed Buddy, my husband, a brochure describing the sort of furnaces he recommended.

"A Honeywell K-970, I'd say, for a house this size. She'll run at 100,000 BTU and probably gut gas bills a good thirty percent. Or you could go the 990 route. A bit more pricey. But its thermostat is iPhone compatible." The repairman turned to me as if I'd be impressed by that. "You can turn it on by remote. Starts warming the house before anyone gets home." For a moment, I misheard and thought he'd said *warning* instead of *warming* and wondered what he'd meant by that.

There is a 500 dollar price difference between the 970 and the 990. The phone app seems like a gimmick to me, not something we really need. But Buddy likes the idea, especially since he's the one often arriving home early these days and sits in a cold house waiting for it to warm.

"Plus," Buddy added, after thoroughly reading the brochure and online reviews, "it'll track our consumption patterns. It's got graphs. And notifications. The app displays any problems or inefficiencies we have."

That seems like a stretch to me. We are already pretty good at conserving heat — sealing windows in the winter, lowering the thermostat at night and whenever we're out. And, with the boys away at college and traveling summers, they're not around to fiddle with the controls. But 970 or 990 — the fate of the old furnace is sealed. It's on its way out, going wherever old furnaces go. I just want to give it one last look over before it's dismantled and hauled off.

The old furnace does not sit flush in the corner. You can squeeze behind it. The boys, when they were young, got frightened by a raccoon hiding there. She had apparently fallen through a basement window while searching for a warm place to nest. Strange noises were coming from the basement. After a quick look, the boys came running up the steps yelling, "There's a ghost down there! For real. A ghost!"

Years later, we discovered one of the boys had been hiding small bags of marijuana inside an unscrewed air vent. Not just a little. Several bags, along with rolling paper and a Hearth 'n Kettle matchbook. Both boys denied it, but eventually Jamie told on his brother Casey. He said Casey'd been selling it at school. He was disciplined, of course.

"You could have killed us all," Buddy told him, seemingly more concerned about the matches than the marijuana. "Do you realize how dangerous it is to strike a match close to a gas furnace? You're grounded for the next two weeks. And not one peep about it."

I kept the book of matches as a reminder to be more watchful. Buddy supposedly flushed the marijuana down the toilet and into the septic tank. But, now that I think about it, I wouldn't be surprised if he'd kept some and smoked it from time to time before the kids and I arrived home.

If I knew the language of furnaces, I'm sure the old beast could tell me a thing or two about my family, things I don't already know. It has lived with us for decades, converting cool, poisonous gas into nurturing heat, pumping it like ventricles into every crevice and corner of our house. It knows us all too well. It will be strange when it's gone and some new machine assumes its place.

There it stands. Quiet and nearly lifeless. Inside, the pilot light still burns, but no longer ignites reliably. At least the leak has been sealed. A small leak, I learned, can allow gas to invisibly accumulate. Inhalation, over time, can cause stress to the immune system, dizziness, sinus pain, depression, memory loss. Even madness.

I run the Eveready light along the metal ducts and panels. A bottom right corner is covered with aluminium tape, a temporary patch placed by the repairman to cover a hole. Critters, he said, could crawl right in. He'd seen plenty of mice, rats, squirrels and moles make winter homes for themselves in such gaps.

Above me, the light beam catches upon silver threads running between rafters — spider webs with their white egg sacs that neither Buddy nor the repairman bothered to brush away. I step closer. I aim the light beneath the furnace. Dark grey balls of bushy lint and dozens of dead rolly polies curled into pellets cover the enamel floor. The once-red tiles, blackened with soot, now bear dull gouges and scrape marks.

Whoosh! The blue-tongued pilot light ignites into an orange radiance. The cinder-block walls are set aglow. Heat pricks my cheeks and eyelids. And in that very instance, a figure appears. She is standing opposite the furnace, watching me. I barely glimpse her face before the flame quits and she slips into darkness.

Trying too quickly to back away, I bang my head against a metal shaft. Hard enough that the joining comes loose. I cry out. There is no one home to hear. My pulse gallops. Feathery lights float upon my retina. I press a hand against the back of my head. The hair is damp with sweat or blood or some liquid that has drained from the shaft above.

I back further away, still pointing the Eveready toward the furnace, waiting for something to move. I call out, "Hello?" "Hello," I repeat. I imagine observing myself from the outside. A clumsy woman inspecting an old furnace, imagining something ghost-like. A ridiculous, laughable woman with an unruly imagination.

Much of life is laughable if you gain enough perspective. My own is no less laughable than any other. Certainly no less laughable than Buddy's, with his erratic fancies. Acrylic painting one month. Improv workshops the next. Vipassana meditation. Hatha yoga. That lasted a week before his back gave out. Took Vicodin for the next three months. Why wasn't he home now, anyway? Oh right. Out until nine. *Mindfulness teacher training* at Brisby. So he says.

The furnace clicks off again. The flame, starved of gas, makes a little *chirp* as it goes out. "Your furnace shuts down too quick," the repairman explained. "It runs too hot, which makes the heat sensor switch the gas off." This I can understand. This is something the old furnace and I share in common. Too much of anything and we shut down.

There is a slow, unwinding whir as something in the furnace dies to a halt. All is quiet for a moment. Just the sound of breath passing in and out my nostrils.

Then a loud thump startles me. It reverberates as though an aluminium shaft has been kicked.

"Hello? Is someone there?"

Sometimes you need to play out your fears. You know it's only your imagination running hot, creating illusions. But what's the harm in following it through if no one is there to watch or judge?

"I know you're there," I say, dragging the beam of light back and forth along the grey cinder block wall.

If you only act crazy when alone, by yourself, and completely sane when other people are around, are you actually crazy? Of course not. Who doesn't imagine horrible things in the dark? Phantoms are brought to life through deprivation of the senses.

"Who are you?" I plead, trying to draw the girl out of hiding. "Say something or I'll call the police."

I slide one foot forward. There is a sound like air flowing through a pipe or the expiration of a long, steady breath.

"My husband will be home any minute."

I struggle to hold the light steady with one hand while reaching into my back pants pocket for the phone. Not to call the police — I would not risk embarrassing myself like that — but for the camera. If she reappears, I will have proof. A photo of the girl. *See, I'm not crazy. There she is. Can you see? Those eyes? Those teeth? That impish grin? Now tell me that's just my imagination.*

I raise the phone to observe the furnace through its touch screen. The image is dim and grainy. Sensors struggle to calibrate the correct aperture. Pixels adjust until the image onscreen is more visible than through the naked eye. Rusted rivet heads are revealed. Spangle patterns appear upon the aluminium casing. A dark oilcloth exposed between grating slats.

Yet the more details displayed, the less I trust what I see, as if the surfeit of information conceals what I sense is really there, invisible, coursing like blood through its veins. Strange how we allow such contraptions into our homes. Lethal powers held at bay by only a few tubes and wires. How can we trust they will not turn against us, betray us? Even during its final days, this old furnace retains its god-like power to nurture or annihilate, warm or enflame.

I reach into my pocket, search for the book of matches. The holy book of Hearth 'n Kettle. All it would take is one strike, a raised red tip held to the pale blue tongue of the gas line, and all our failings will be forgiven.

The Black Bag

There's no way I will get a story written during this flight. Why even try? The flight attendant will keep interrupting. Turbulence will make my handwriting illegible. Hunger, stale air and cabin pressure will leave me too groggy to complete a thought. The seat back in front of me will grind into my kneecaps. The toddler in row 19 will crap his pants. The Finnish guy beside me will snore, drool sliding off his double chin and onto the armrest. There are too many distractions on board to allow one's imagination to truly soar.

Even as I write this simple confession of my inability to write, the Finn beside me leans forward, gazes at my scribbles and says, Are you a writer? Are you writing a story?

No, I say, I am not a writer. I'm only trying to jot down some notes, some personal thoughts.

It is too bad you are not a writer, says the Finn, because I had a strong experience that can make a very good story.

Yes, I'm sure you did, I think. Most non-writers believe it's all that simple. The slightest blip on the radar of ordinary experience instantly qualifies as a story, so they believe, as if stories were solely about unique experiences. They have no understanding that even the most mundane moments in human life — dissolving wafers in a cup of tea, riding a shopping mall escalator or diapering a baby — these simple, every-day matters can be brought to life on the page in a way that transcends the quotidian and conveys our most esoteric feelings, beliefs and ideas.

But I don't have a chance to explain any of this to the Finn who has decided to inflict his recent experiences upon me — even if I insist I am not a writer.

I should be on this flight *yesterday*, he says, jabbing a fat Finn finger into the seat back in front of him. Yesterday, I am at this airport early. I stand in line. I give them ticket. Then two security men — they say, *Come with us*. What is this, I am thinking? I have good visa, all my paperwork...

He wipes his face on a shirt sleeve, then leans closer until I see those swelling pores on his pink Finn nose oozing perspiration.

These men take me to a small room. There is only one table and one chair. They tell me, sit. I wait. I wait a *loooooo*ng time. Then two different men come to me. They want to hear all what I do for work, how long I travel, who are my parents — yes, all of this.

Long story short, they make mistake. They confuse me with another Henrik Vaara from Turku who, I think, is in very big trouble. But this is not my problem. My problem is I miss my flight. The airline say to me this is not their problem. They say this is problem because of police. But they give me new ticket and pay for hotel room.

The Finn pauses as the flight attendant takes drink orders.

Please, may I have two Coca-Cola?

Two? repeats the flight attendant.

Yes. I am so sorry. I have very big thirst.

The flight attendant passes me an orange juice, then hands Henrik two Coke cans and a cup of ice. Henrik continues.

Okay. So I have big inconvenience at airport. What can I say? I take shuttle bus to hotel. I watch *Friends* on TV. I fall sleeping watching *As Good as It Gets*. Do you know this film? You will tell to me how it ends, maybe, please.

So I am sleeping. Then there is big noise. Some *bang bang*. Someone in my room, I think. I try not to make any breathing, like I am invisible. This person — they can keep my bag, take my computer — I don't care. Only don't kill me. Right?

The light goes on and this person and I both have big shock. It is some pretty, business woman with — oh, I don't know — she is carrying so many bags.

I am room 228, she say to me. Is this room 228?

This room is 228, I say.

We are both confused. She say she will have hotel manager fix this problem. Okay, I say. No problem.

I try to sleep. Maybe sleep for three hours. Maybe four. I wake up. I am ready to leave and — what is this? Beside my door is some black bag. It is from this business woman, I am thinking.

Henrik has only just finished his first Coke and is already a bit twitchy. Dandruff flutters from his jerky eyebrows. He burps and lifts the end of his navy tie to wipe his purply lips. He continues.

Something in me wants to look inside this bag. What is this word? *Curiosity*. Yes. So I open bag and what do I find? I find little — what do you call these? Small white clouds for making away ladies cosmetics? Cotton balls! Yes. A bag of cotton balls. And! And a white plastic container with big yellow sticker. It say *Danger haze-artist materials*. Or something like this.

This black bag, I am thinking, is big problem for me. If I leave bag, some cleaning woman say it is mine. Maybe they call airline and make trouble for me. But if I bring bag to hotel desk and explain, they maybe call police and police want me to stay, answer questions, sign papers — this sort of thing.

But I cannot miss flight, you see. Not for second time. So, I think, maybe I leave bag in hallway, right? But this is also problem. People *everywhere*. All leaving same time. Someone see me for sure if I leave black bag in hallway.

Okay, I think. New plan. I sit in hotel lobby. I put bag behind chair. I wait. I wait. I am thinking — *Pfft*.

Henrik walks two fingers through the air.

I walk away, he whispers. I leave bag. Nobody think this is my bag. I just go. But when I stand I see security camera. And camera is watching me. What do I do now? Nothing. I take bag and leave hotel.

Henrik quickly scans the isle, the back heads of passengers and the overhead bins. He lowers his voice to a whisper again and rests a finger upon my drink tray.

Now this is where I am getting very nervous, because on shuttle bus to airport...

Maybe the altitude is affecting me. Maybe the cabin pressure is low. I don't know. Maybe I'm too hungry to focus on what the Finn is telling me. My attention wanders. My eye is drawn to the window, past the Finn's left shoulder. There are billowy cloud tops. Cotton balls afflicted with gigantism. In the distance they dissolve into pale blue sky, like thoughts into...

No, stories will not come to me here, not with so many distractions. How can anyone coax their deepest self from the shadows of subconscious thought when complete strangers assail their privacy? How are stories to form in such an invasive environment? If only I were alone somewhere quiet. If only there wasn't this plane, this flight attendant, the oceanic roar of air vents, and this large Finn beside me, yammering on and on as if he had a story to tell.

Five-Headed Satan

Five-Headed Satan lives on the ground floor. No one likes him, not a single one of his five heads. He is noisy and unsocial. Odd smells waft from his apartment and down the hall, sometimes even up the stairwell. He is often in the foyer, on his way to the cellar where he rents a storage unit. Gravy, another tenant living on the ground floor, says the satan is digging a hole in his storage unit, trying to reach Hell. It is unlikely he will get far. The satan is tall, but fairly scrawny for someone with so many heads. Thin arms and bony wrists. It would take him decades to dig a hole deep enough to get anywhere.

I am a milliner. I make hats. An anachronistic profession in this day and age, but I swear it will soon make a comeback. We are verging on a new age of uncompromising, artisanal craftsmanship. People really do prefer quality, handmade goods. And once you've experienced a proper hat you can't settle for anything less.

I have a good relationship with four high-end department stores. Two downtown. One in Tokyo. Another in Dubai, of all places. Making hats does not make me rich, but it brings in enough money to afford a decent apartment in a good part of town with a large, sunny workspace. I get paid on consignment, so it's often feast or famine. My peak season is December. During the holidays, I live large. Come summer, I scrape by. It's then I look around at people wearing baseball caps made of nylon and plastic and I start to lose heart. What is it with these people? Think how much nicer they would look and feel in a fine chambray trilby, or a slouchy knit beanie, or a floppy brimmed sun bonnet, or a ruffled crocheted muffy.

Betsy is the woman I'm in love with. She is a sales girl at Nordstrom. We have been seeing each other for nearly five months and it has gotten quite serious. We've already covered topics such as baby names, wedding cake flavors, invitation fonts, joint bank accounts and communicable diseases. (Hadley, lemon, Garamond, joint, cold sores.) All that's left is to propose. She's waiting, I know. But she will also expect a ring. Not necessarily a diamond. Sapphire may be acceptable. But at the moment, not even moissanite and zirconia are in my price range.

Then it struck me. Five hats. That's all I would need. Sell an extra five hats this month and Bob's your uncle. I would have enough cash to purchase a proper engagement ring and Betsy's betrothal would be mine.

I stood outside the satan's door trying to work up enough courage to knock. It smelled of sulphur, rotting meat and cherry cola. Warm air gushed from beneath the door, along with flakes of dust and ash. Voices intoned from within. Not five voices, just two.

One spoke, the other repeated.

"Hollow Pox"

"Hollow Pox"

"Trowel Hammer"

"Trowel Hammer"

"Arbor Nemesis"

"Arbor Nemesis"

"Fruit Compote"

"Fruit Compote"

This liturgy went on for several minutes. I thought maybe I should leave and come back later. But then I thought, *Betsy*. My Betsy. I could envision her oval face, her smile, her ruby dimples, the tight blonde curls, her ever-so-faint acne scars. I was doing this for her. For us. Our future together. Till death do us part. I mustn't be cowardly. I raised my fist and knocked.

There was silence. After a lengthy pause, the door swung open. It was just a man. A bald, single-headed man wearing a rumpled suit. He held a wool topcoat over one arm and carried a leather briefcase. He glared at me without speaking as he walked past.

A voice cried from within the dark interior. "Yes?!" Then another, higher voice. "Who is it?" Five-Headed Satan stepped into the light. He was much taller than I remembered. He stooped so his five heads did not quite touch the ceiling. All five peered down at me with flickering eyes. I fumbled for words, momentarily forgetting why I had come. I raised my portfolio and unsnapped the cover.

"What's that you have?" a third, gravely voice spoke. "Let's see. Bring it here."

I did what he commanded and stepped into the room. Floorboards creaked beneath my Venetian loafers, no rug or carpeting to muffle their groan.

"I'm Nick. From upstairs, third floor. Down the hall on the left. Sorry to interrupt. I can come back if this is inconvenient."

"No worries. Come in."

"Come in. Come in," repeated a different voice. "Yes, do," said another.

The windows were shuttered and covered in dark, heavy cloth. A shaded floor lamp cast a pinkish glow, illuminating the room's furnishings — a wood-trimmed sofa, two matching armchairs and a hefty Georgian coffee table. All facing a large brick hearth, with an artificial fire glowing beneath a marble mantelpiece. Orange and yellow flames spun slowly like a rotisserie within the ceramic birch logs.

I held my portfolio like a defensive shield, ready in case the satan should make a sudden lunge toward me.

"What's that you got, mate?"

My eyes adjusted to the dim interior. I saw more clearly the towering figure with its many, varying faces.

"I'm a mi mi mi milliner," I stammered. "I m-make the best hats you'll find anywhere. On Earth, that is. Hand-made. I have a studio upstairs. It's where I work. Everyone loves my hats." I sounded like an imbecile. It would be easier to show him the studio. Invite him upstairs. But inviting the satan over was out of the question. What would people say? Cavorting with demons? Word gets around. Such things are not good for business. In this town, especially. Maybe in Paris it would be different.

I stepped closer. I opened my case. I'm proud of my work and I've spent a great deal of time getting my portfolio just right. A few of the photos I snapped myself, but most shots were professionally taken by one of the city's top still life photographers. Good studio lighting and narrow depth of focus offer a dramatic display and high-end presentation. I held the book open and turned through the pages, watching the heads for their reactions.

"Closer!" commanded one of the five.

I stepped forward. "Please." He gestured toward a chair with his clawed hand. My body sank into the seat cushion, releasing a cloud of dust and mildew.

The satan shuffled toward the sofa. A long skinny tail dragged behind him, drawing a dark line through the dust. He adjusted his tail before sitting, then leaned forward with all five heads.

"Now, let's see."

He tapped a claw upon the coffee table.

I laid down the portfolio, turning it to face the satan. His sharp nail slowly dragged over each page before raising the bottom corner. With each turn of the page he expired a foul steam from the depth of his bowels. The smell made me dizzy. I was glad to be seated, otherwise I may have lost balance or fainted.

"Hold on a sec'," said one head. "Turn back."

His hands flipped back to a page featuring a distinguished narrow-brimmed homburg. One of my great triumphs. A masterpiece composed of eight different grades of angora. I had flown to Vancouver to select the actual rabbits employed in the felting process.

"No, next page. One more back."

He turned the page again, this time to a beaded tea-green bonnet of silk-covered buckram with Champagne ribbon and ivory lace. "Who is that!" exclaimed one head. "*Mamma mia!*" cried another. A third head whistled a wolf call.

The photo was of Betsy, one I'd taken when we first met, before we began dating. It was the only time I'd persuaded her to model for me. "Just my hair and forehead," she said. "I don't want people seeing it's me." In the end, I could not bring myself to crop that lovely face and had it printed as is.

"I'd be pleased to meet her," said the head, far left. "Can it be arranged?"

"Yes, let's!" said another.

"We must!"

I was lost for words. My lips moved but no sound emerged. I inhaled sharply before responding. "Sorry. You have the wrong idea. She's only a model. That's one of my hats she's wearing. You see, that's what I'm here for. To show you hats. I thought maybe you would like one. Or five. Custom made. Any style you prefer."

"Hats!?"

The heads thought for a moment. Each repeated the word "hat," drawing it out as if it had more than one syllable. They slowly began to smile. Five eerie, deeply unsettling smiles.

"Great idea!"

"I'd love one!"

"I'd love you to have one."

"I'd love us all to have one."

"Better to look at a pretty hat than your filthy scalp."

"Indeed."

"Yes, quite."

They began vigorously flipping through pages, agreeing and disagreeing on various styles and impressions. They wanted something classy, yet with a certain solidity. "Menacing is our style," said one head. "But with swagger," insisted another. "Nothing *fru fru*," added a third. "Righteous," said a fourth. The fifth merely snickered.

"What would you suggest?" asked the center head.

I directed the satan toward my black homburg. "One of my favorites," I said. "And quite menacing. I could alter the brim to add more shadow over the eyes. And augment the band with a patinated, skull-shaped clasp."

"How much?" asked the middle head, his thick black brows lowering, suspiciously.

I carefully explained how I sourced my materials, the labor involved in sculpting felt, sizing, adhering brims, hand stitching, etc. I emphasized the enormous care and patience that goes into each and every hat before quoting him a price with a not inconsiderable margin. I shrewdly added, "Since you will be needing five hats and because you are a good neighbor, I will gladly discount your order by ten percent."

The heads all nodded in agreement and whispered amongst themselves.

"What about red? Can we get them in red?"

"Of course. Any color you like."

"And velvet, not felt," added another.

"Yes, that's possible. I work with velvet from time to time. But fine, quality velvet is quite pricey."

"How much are we talking then for, say, five of these *hombreros*?"

I gave the satan a new price, much higher this time. He did not blink. Not one eye out of ten.

"Yes. Very good," said the middle head. They all nodded in consent. "We'll take five *homburgers* in red velvet. We'll pay full price. No discount. Full price. We insist."

I had expected to be haggled down a good thirty or forty percent, to tell the truth, which is often the case when dealing with buyers. This was far more than I'd hoped. A windfall. A lucky day. Oh my! *Oh Betsy! Forget sapphire, we're going for diamond!*

"One condition," added the satan. "We'd like to meet the young lady." His hands flipped back through the portfolio and aimed a dark, pointy claw at Betsy's chin. "Can you please extend our invitation?"

"He's very nice. Not at all what you'd expect from a five-headed satan."

"Nick! I am not going to visit your satan friend."

"He's not my friend. He's just a neighbor downstairs. Really, there's nothing to be worried about. He only wants to meet you."

"It seems weird."

"Betsy, the guy is loaded. He could be a big help to you. To us. Get on his good side. He might become your most loyal customer."

Nordstrom was putting the screws to Betsy. Sales had been down ever since she took over Men's Suits and Formal Wear. Her commissions were forty percent lower than they'd been in Ladies Hosiery and Lace.

Jerry, the tailor, sat idly on his stool all day glaring at her — as if that would help matters! She came home most days in tears.

"Do you know what you could charge for a five-collared Burberry dress shirt?"

She bit into her lower lip, then spoke. "How many arms does this five-headed satan have?"

"Two. Just two."

"Well, that's good. I'm not sure Jerry could add arms. He'd have to go to a place like Savile Row for that sort of thing."

"There is a tail though," I added. "But you'd only need to split a hole in the pant seam."

"Nick, I still don't understand. Why does he want to meet me?"

"He liked your photo. He thought you looked beautiful. And kind. And he's just a lonely old satan. You'd be cheering him up. There's no harm in it. I'll be right there with you."

Betsy reluctantly agreed and we arranged to meet Thursday during her lunch break to visit Five-Headed Satan.

I spent Thursday morning on Treacher Street considering fabric samples. Five-Headed Satan had asked for "classy." A red velvet homburg was anything but that. I didn't argue, though. If red velvet was what he wanted, that's what I'd make.

There were approximately fifty shades of red at Schmalbergs, from barn to scarlet, ruby to blood. I sorted through the immense fabric bolts. The sales girl snipped samples. I laid them side by side beneath an

LED lamp to determine their true color. I narrowed my selection to five, including crimson and, my favorite, carmine, a hue which split the difference between ruby and incarnadine. The sales girl bound the samples into a small book. I thanked her, then hurried to Nordstrom to fetch Betsy.

"I'm nervous," Betsy said, stepping out of the cab. "Is this a good idea?"

"Trust me. The old guy appears more imposing than he really is. After a while you don't notice all those heads. I mean, you do. But you don't. You know what I mean?"

"No, not really."

She took my hand and we walked into the lobby, then down the hall past apartments 4 and 5, until we reached 6. I hadn't noticed it before; someone had gouged two extra sixes beside the door number.

"Ready?"

Betsy straightened her skirt. I knocked and we waited. I knocked a second time. After a moment, floorboards began to creak. Their groans grew louder until the latch clicked and the door swung open. There he was. The satan. He wore a shiny, red cape and a ten-lapeled dinner jacket that fell over his pearl white cummerbund. His black trousers bore mauve grosgrain strips along the side seams. White ash clung to his cuffs. The hairs on every head glistened with styling gel. His necks each wore a different ascot, ranging in colors from auburn to violet.

"Welcome. Please come in. I've prepared a little lunch. I hope you like spinach quiche."

Betsy bravely stepped inside. But as I attempted to enter the apartment, Five-Headed Satan blocked my way. His five heads smiled. "Thank you, Nick. We are looking forward to our hats." He held the door, waiting for me to depart.

"I brought samples," I said, taking the fabric book from my pocket. "I want to get the perfect shade of red before we —"

Five-Headed Satan interrupted. "I don't mean to be rude, Nick," said one head. "But right now we don't want to talk business. We'd just like to get to know your friend."

"That's right," said another head. "A quiet conversation over lunch with Betsy. I hope you understand."

"You can choose a red for us," said another. "Whatever you suggest. We have complete faith in your judgement."

"That's right," reiterated the middle head. "Complete faith in your judgement, Nick."

The five heads nodded in assent. I peered beyond the satan. Betsy was already seated on the sofa. She picked up a coffee table magazine and appeared captivated by whatever was inside its glossy fold-out pages.

"Betsy?" Betsy raised her eyes. "I'll be right upstairs if you need anything, honey."

Betsy shrugged. The five heads smiled. I smiled, too, not sure what more to say.

The door swung shut, sweeping a cloud of dust and ash onto the hall carpet. I adjusted my eyes to the incandescent lights. Beneath their glowing tungsten, my color samples were nearly impossible to differentiate. I flipped the pages. Which was scarlet? Which was berry? Which brick, carmine, coral or blood?

52

Clam Neck Beach

Ray sits on the passenger side. He waits for Edna to return from errands. On warm summer days, he keeps the windows cranked low for air. He cranes his neck to watch passersby and keeps an eye out for parking attendants and ticketers. Delivery workers scuttle past with dollies and satchels. Manual laborers chomp fast food from take-out containers while seated in 4-wheel drive trucks and customized work vans. Teenage girls spoon frozen yogurt out of paper cups. Skateboarders skid down metal handrails and over cement curbs. Ray rests his eyes. He nods off, chin close to his chest. He dreams until, inevitably, an SUV pulls too close or a chopper revs past or an indignant car horn blares like an air raid siren.

Edna returns with each procurement. A handful of junk mail from the P. O. Box. Plastic sacks with frozen dinners, toilet paper and egg cartons. A tray of fresh berries. A white pharmacy bag, receipt stapled to the fold. Each day's errands end with a visit to Clam Neck Beach. They park close to the boardwalk. They sip bottled ice tea and watch the surf.

A few 'Would you believe's or 'For Christ's sake's' sputter from Edna's lips as the car radio transmits one call-in talk show after another. *Caller from Davenport*: "The mainstream media's in on it. There's the problem." *Caller from Hollyoke*: "I know for a fact, exotic dancers been on the White House payroll for years." *Next caller, you're on.* "I'm Anthony. First time caller, long time maverick."

"Check your cap," Edna says.

"My what?"

"The cap for your tea, Ray. See if you've won. They have some sort of sweepstakes. You could win us an Orlando vacation."

Ray examines the seat cushion and floor below his sneakers. He cannot recollect where the bottle cap went.

"Check under your seat, Ray."

Ray does not want to look under the seat. He's not even sure it's physically possible to bend over that far.

"Never mind," Edna says, annoyed. She opens the driver side door and sets foot on the blacktop. The car rocks side to side as she rises. She shuts the door and sticks her face back through the open window. "I'm going to check the water," she says.

Edna in her bright white Reeboks strides across the pavement and onto the boardwalk. Ray watches her disappear as she steps down the berm. A couple minutes later she reappears on the distant sand, her unlaced shoes in one hand. She walks slowly, unsteady, as she makes her way toward the shoreline and the froth of an incoming tide.

Ray and Edna often came to Clam Neck when they first dated. It had once been a popular family beach, but Hurricane Dennis tore up the breakers. It washed away two motels, the Ice Cream Barn and the Pirate's Cove putt putt course. Most families stopped coming, preferring Winslow Beach after that.

At night, Ray and Edna would park in the empty lot. They'd switch the ignition to battery and listen to WCIB as they kissed and groped, fondling each other's bodies over pleats, flannels, gingham and blue denim.

Once, a policeman snuck up on them. He beamed a flashlight through the driver-side window, hoping to catch them by surprise. They were only kissing, though. He rapped a fat knuckle against the glass and shouted, "Get a move on, you two." He pointed toward the gate. They were unnerved, but also excited to have been caught. What might have happened if he'd found them in a more compromising position? Would he have taken down their names, filed a report, stood and watched?

By the end of that summer, they'd begun to leave the parked car. They followed dark trails through the beach grass. Moonlight reflected off dunes, leaving opaque shadows behind them. Edna and Ray spread Indian blankets in these dark hollows. They blindly undressed. Their sparsely lit flesh appeared more thrillingly to each other, more exposed, than ever in broad daylight.

Sometimes they were sole survivors on a barren planet. Sometimes pirate and island savage. Sometimes doctor and patient. Sometimes gangster and moll. Sometimes private dick and *femme fatale* or prison warden and sassy jailbird. Sometimes Cold War spies, raven and swallow. Once, a French trapper and his Indian bride. Another time, they imitated Richard Chamberlain and Rachel Ward as priest and paramour in their favorite miniseries, The Thorn Birds.

On still nights, they heard only the sounds of their own damp bodies, their pounding hearts, and the incessant waves that pulled upon the shoreline. Occasionally, there were voices. A couple strolling the beach. A posse of boisterous teens jangling six-packs. The chime of metal dog tags. An owner's voice crying, "Here, boy!"

A large black hound once sniffed them out. They hadn't heard him approach. He appeared out of nowhere, baring teeth, barking like mad. Ray quickly dismounted and pulled the blanket over them both. Edna could not contain her laughter.

Ray must have dozed off. He straightens his back and peers out the window. The sky has grown a few shades darker, a blooming pink horizon suffused over a purple sea. More cars are parked along the edge of the blacktop. Two scavenging gulls circle overhead. One dives toward a plastic Chipwich wrapper tumbling across asphalt.

Down on the beach, Ray spots a small knot of people. They're gathered around a figure lying in the sand. They seem to be simply looking at the body, quietly observing and nothing more.

Ray's stomach clenches. His heart flops in his chest and knocks against his ribcage. His hands tremble. There's no doubt it's Edna lying there on the sand. He does not know how he knows this, but he knows it as clearly as he knows he is awake and not dreaming.

He pulls the door handle and pushes against the upholstery with his right elbow and shoulder. His feet topple onto the pavement. He rises, steadying himself on the doorframe. Pulling the seat release, he leans into the back. Ligaments and joints snap and pop as he reaches for his walking cane.

Edna and Ray once took CPR lessons. Everyone did back then. The boat club held classes at the start of each summer. You were given a pamphlet and tested on a wax canvas dummy that tasted of lye soap and smelled like old socks.

Afterwards, Edna and Ray practiced on each other. Calling their make-out sessions "practice" was sort of a joke. But only half a joke. They thought, *This is strange but real. You could actually save someone's life this way.*

They blew air back and forth between each other's mouths until there was so much life swelling within themselves, it seemed they might burst open if they did not rush to Clam Neck beach, dive behind the dunes and release all that quaking ardor held inside.

After they married, Edna and Ray worked together at Package Liquors on Route 6. They put in long hours. The drive to Clam Neck began to feel too far, especially in the irritatingly slow summer traffic.

The business had once belonged to Edna's father, but he'd retired, leaving it for the two of them to run. They worked it alone, sharing the same 12-hour shift. Evenings, they were so worn out, they could do nothing more than drive home, order Dominos pizza and watch movies on TV.

They were saving money. They had plans. They would buy a Florida condo, like Edna's father had done. Retire early. They'd spend their days by the sea, enjoy winter and summer on the white, sandy shoreline. They'd sail, sunbathe, collects shells and driftwood. Ray would grill bluefish and cobia on an outdoor bar-b-que. Edna would blender fresh-picked citrus into smoothies. It was a good plan. It would have worked, too, if Ray hadn't gotten ill. And the medical bills hadn't bled nearly all their savings.

Ray is now very awake, aware of everything around him, every hovering dandelion seed, every propelling leaf, the swirls of sand upon blacktop, the cawing of gulls, the distant highway rush, the rattling bayberry branches.

The sea roils in Ray's ear canal. The undertow gurgles, like a gas pump. His twisty, grey nostril hairs quiver as they detect blooms of algae in the distant sea foam and rotting crab shells in the dry grass.

Ray propels his way across the parking lot, the rubber tip of his cane pumping like a spring. He keeps pace with two interlocked dragonflies buzzing beside him. He speeds past the dragonflies as he bounds onto the boardwalk. In his mind he is sprinting. His chest heaves. Perspiration dampens his shirt back. Suspenders cut into his shoulders. Long neglected muscles in his calves and thighs are summoned to life, responding eagerly, as if happy to be called to purpose once again.

From the top of the steps, Ray sees more clearly. The body below is large and on its back. Someone is holding a cellphone. Another peers toward the horizon. The water is choppy. Whitecaps break apart the dark surface. Rusty orange clouds roil toward shore.

Ray loses his footing on the top steps. Time slows. The dragonflies halt their aerial fornication. Their massive globular eyes marvel at Ray's lofty plummet. Ray experiences a sense of detachment: self from body, limbs from torso. He watches one shoe fall free. His cane revolves in slow motion. Both legs circle overhead, exchange lead, then land before the rest of his body onto the sand.

He may have blacked out for a moment. Surprisingly, there is no pain. He gropes for his glasses, which have landed somewhere out of sight. They cannot be found. He gives up and rises to his feet. He sets off again toward the crowd, managing to push on without cane, left shoe or clear vision.

Someone in the group appears to be looking his way, raising an arm. One by one, the others turn in Ray's direction. He knows his movements are out of sync. Hands, elbows, knees, feet — all working as if under separate operating instructions. His momentum is unstoppable, though. Heart beating loud, louder than even the tinnitus in his left ear. Sand lodges between his gums and embeds within waves of hair, jowls and wrinkles. Specks flutter from his bushy grey brows as he leans into the wind.

He wants to cry out, *Hang in there Edna! I'm coming!* But there is not enough air in his lungs to both shout and run. A voice in his head speaks to him.

Breathe, damnit. Breathe. It's what they used to say to each other. A private joke. Lying on the shore. Rolling one atop the other into the surf. Waves lapping at their bodies. Kelp caught in Edna's long copper hair. He pinches her nose. She pinches his. *Breathe,* they would whisper between breaths. *Breathe,* they'd repeat, giddily blowing air back and forth past fluttering lips and into each other's open mouths.

Two Tourists

For hours they lay awake listening to words spoken beyond the inadequate partition. Some were mumbled. Some came out multi-syllabically. Some grunted into existence. *Jesus. Angel. Open. Baby. Faster. Monkey. Do it. Harder. Yes. Now. Pillow.* Mrs. Joanna Smyth rolled onto her side and adjusted the pension bed pillow, as if the word *pillow* had been spoken specifically to her.

"Shhh," whispered Mr. Thomas Smyth.

"I didn't say anything."

"You're squeaking the bed."

"Oh for Pete's," she whispered. "I'm not going to *not* squeak."

Mr. Thomas Smyth rolled his eyes and resumed listening to the couple beyond the partition. They were speaking in nearly full sentences once more.

"Those are my nipples," said the woman.

"Them's mine now," said her companion.

We shouldn't be listening, thought Mrs. Smyth, *but if they're going to talk this way they don't deserve privacy.*

"You know what I liked best about today?" The woman's hushed words came crackling from deep within her throat.

"The funicular ride?"

"No. When I jerked ya off 'eneath the breakie table."

"That was naughty."

"What did people think when they saw your face? You must have looked absolutely hilarious. Sitting there with your orange juice an' corn flakes an' your eyes going mad all up in your head." She snorted a bit as she giggled.

"No one was paying attention. They were all too fascinated with their guidebooks and iphones."

"Bristol," whispered Mrs. Smyth. "Their accent sounds Bristol, I'd say."

The woman mumbled a response they could not discern. "Jacket or jack off," whispered Mr. Smyth, interpreting. Mrs. Smyth thought, perhaps, they were talking about the nylon jackets she and Mr. Smyth wore at breakfast. Matching green windbreakers. *That older couple with their identical, nylon jackets,* They could have been thinking. *That older couple with an enormous video camera and its ludicrously long microphone covered in a sheath of fake fur.*

Mr. Smyth had purchased the camera shortly before their trip. Filmmaking was to become his new hobby. He brought the camera home shortly before their departure. "This is the very camera they shot Season One of The Office with," he said. He'd gotten a good deal buying it used.

"You're not taking that with us, are you?"

"Of course I am. I want to document the entire journey. It will be good practice. I can edit it and turn it into a short film."

"I don't want to be on film," said Mrs. Smyth.

"Oh, c'mon now," he reproached.

Mr. Smyth had so far filmed the changing of the castle guards, floating casino boats, portrait artists atop the Charles Bridge, a blind street musician playing Bach adagios on her flute, a living statue of a man painted entirely silver, a red and yellow tram rattling past an art nouveau palace and, most recently, the svelte, young receptionist, Jana. Jana worked the front desk at the Pension Radost, where the Smyths were staying, a 15-minute tram ride from the city center.

"My wife won't let me film her," Mr. Smyth explained to Jana. "Will you say a few words to the camera?"

"I don't know. What should I say?"

"Welcome to Czechoslovakia. Hope you enjoy the show. Something like that."

"Welcome to Czech Republic," said Jana, smiling for the camera. "I hope you have a very enjoyable visit and great memories."

"That's perfect, Jana. Thank you."

A large thump against the partition knocked the headboard against Mrs. Smyth's head. She winced and let out a small *umph* of irritation. Mr. Smyth, remained staring at the ceiling, unbothered. Mrs. Smyth readjusted her pillow, moving it away from the headboard. As the bed continued to tremble, the man beyond the partition seemed to speak her name.

Mr. Smyth chuckled. "You're hearing what you want to hear, Jo. He clearly said *marijuana* Not *Joanna*."

The man's voice continued. This time Mrs. Smyth heard the man say, "Lovely figure for a woman her age."

"Who do you imagine he's talking about?"

"*Shhh*," whispered Mr. Smyth.

The woman beyond the partition began singing softly — *Hey! I just met you. This is crazy. Here's my number. Call* — her singing abruptly stopped, interrupted by a deep inhale and guttural sigh. The pounding against the partition resumed, causing the Smyth's bed frame to vibrate.

"We should ask Jana to change our rooms tomorrow," whispered Mrs. Smyth.

"What?" asked Mr. Smyth.

"Change our rooms. Tomorrow."

"Eh? I can't hear."

"Tomorrow. Ask Jana —"

Mr. Smyth threw his hand over Mrs. Smyth's mouth. The couple opposite the partition had stopped moving, perhaps having heard Mrs. Smyth calling out the name *Jana*.

They lay still for several moments, listening. The silence beyond the partition gave way to a gentle snoring. The Smyths readjusted their pillows and shut their eyes. Eventually, they too joined their neighbors in sleep.

At breakfast, the Smyths surveyed the dining hall, searching for the couple from the room adjacent to theirs. They felt sure they could identify them with no problem. Their voices made a distinct impression. They were young, in their late twenties. She would be wearing a light cotton gown with multiple strands of beads around her neck and large chunky bracelets circling her thin wrists, thought Mr. Smyth. Mrs. Smyth imagined her in black tights and a long t-shirt with some fashion-design or athletic logo. Perhaps pink trainers on her feet with tongues sewn into the eyelets and no laces. She pictured the young man with a beard, a silver stud in one ear and maybe another over the opposite eye. He would have bright colored pants and don a t-shirt with artwork from his favorite band. Mr. Smyth thought the boy would be smart looking. Thick-framed glasses. Hair combed back. Dark and well groomed stubbles of hair on his jaw and upper lip.

None of the couples in the pension dining room, however, resembled what either imagined. Most were middle-aged couples, much like themselves, with the exception of a group of young Asian women, accompanied by an older man, perhaps their college professor or some sort of chaperone.

"They're not here," said Mrs. Smyth.

"You're right," said Mr. Smyth. "Probably still sleeping."

"But I swore I heard them leave before us. They must have skipped breakfast."

After their black tea, untoasted rye bread, butter and jam the Smyths left the Pension Radost. Mr. Smyth cradled his camera and tripod. Mrs. Smyth shouldered a navy blue rucksack containing an extra fleece, a bag of chocolate-covered almonds and a plastic bottle of *Do-*

brá Voda mineral water. She held the guidebook in one hand so she could read it while riding the 22 tram to the city center.

The guidebook highlighted the astrological clock as one of the city's most impressive sites. According to the guide, a small pageant of mechanical figures moves in and out of windows located beside a clock face that conveys time, seasons, positions of the sun and moon, phases of the zodiac, and every Holy Day throughout the year. Mr. Smyth planned to record the complete, chronographic display on video.

The old 22 rattled its way along the incline. They passed a cathedral square, then a commercial boulevard with sex shops and music bars, before reaching Národní Street. The Smyths exited the tram outside the National Theater and consulted the map Jana had given them. Old Town Square, with its astrological tower, was still several streets beyond the tram line. No rush, though. The clock performed every hour on the hour. They could walk leisurely and film sites along the way.

The Smyths hurried past crowds of tourists with their raised smartphones and digital cameras. Many followed behind umbrella-wielding tour guides. Several girls wearing matching pink t-shirts and white baseball caps glided past on Segway scooters. An African man in a red suit, wearing a renaissance wig of silver curls, offered them both menus bound in blue vinyl. They declined his invitation to enter a nearby "authentic" Czech restaurant.

Upon turning the next corner, the Smyths discovered a picturesque alley of crooked cobblestones, rusty lamps, crumbling orange plaster, and iron-barred windows. Halfway down the alley, Mr. Smyth stopped before a secluded antique shop and began extending the legs of his tripod. The window display was a chaotic mix of leather bound books, Russian cameras, phonograph albums, ceramic kitchen containers, opera glasses, brass horns, disembodied marionette parts and vintage pornography.

"This is the stuff," he said, pressing the red record button.

A few blocks further on, a black and gold, vertical banner caught Mr. Smyth attention. *Sex Museum*, it read.

"Jo, stand next to that sign," said Mr. Smyth, raising the camera to his shoulder and backing across the lane. "I'm not standing there," said Mrs. Smyth. "Oh, come on. Be a love." Mrs. Smyth lowered her head and walked away.

Mr. Smyth slowly stepped forward and into the museum. His lens zoomed past arches and pillars, focusing upon two full-size, torso-shaped lamps. Each bore a strap-on phallus, resembling a giant light switch. The ticket vendor turned toward Mr. Smyth. Her corseted chest rose and fell with a sigh.

Mr. Smyth finished filming and hurried to catch up with Mrs. Smyth, who was just then entering a congested stream of tourists at the cross street. They walked together towards the city's crowded main square and stood beneath the clocktower. While waiting for the hour to strike, Mrs. Smyth reread her guidebook and Mr. Smyth adjusted his tripod, trying to raise the camera over the many heads gathered to view the clock's complicated and colorful display.

Mrs. Smyth read out loud, "*Upon completion of the original clock*, it says here, *its maker was blinded by the town council. Never again would he be able to replicate the orloj. For this cruelty, the blind clockmaker sought revenge. He entered the tower late one night and smashed his magnificent creation. It took a hundred years before another clock maker could grasp the secrets of its mechanism and restore the clock to working order.*"

Mrs. Smyth peered up from her guide book. She sought out the mechanical figures. The skeleton was the first to catch her eye. It held a bell and hammer. It shared a platform with a turban-headed Turk, meant to symbolize sensual pleasure — or so the guide book asserted. Opposite those two stood another pairing of figures: a hook-nosed Jewish moneychanger with a sack of gold and, beside him, a well-coiffed man staring into a hand mirror, symbolizing vanity.

The hand-held mirror lurched toward the man's face. Simultaneously, a bell clanged throughout the square. Each mechanical figure jumped to life. Arms swung, bodies lurched, heads twisted side to side as if all were replying *No!* to the mechanical skeleton's clanging death knell.

Mrs. Smyth turned to her husband. "Are you getting it?" Mr. Smyth, with one eye pressed to the viewfinder, waved at her to hush.

The shuttered windows beside the clock face sprang open. Miniature apostles, one by one, moved behind each window, pausing briefly to face the crowd. Hundreds of tourists, heads tilted back, gazed upon the display. Many were taking their own videos and photographs. They stared at tiny screens held between fingers and palms. Mrs. Smyth overheard a woman nearby speaking in an Australian accent. "Horology, my dear, is the study of time, not whores."

As they left Old Town Square, walking past the gothic spires of Týn Cathedral, a voice called out Mrs. Smyth's name. "Joanna!" She turned. A man in light blue trousers and burgundy v-neck sweater was hastily approaching. His face was puffy and pink. She vaguely recognized the man, though she struggled to recall from where. As he stopped to catch his breath, she realized he was a boy she had once known. A boy from her school years, but now much older.

"Of all places — "

"Robert," said Mrs. Smyth, the name springing back to mind. "Do you live here?"

Robert smiled. "Of course not. I'm on holiday like everyone else. Isn't it lovely? Third time I've been here. No, fifth, actually."

Mrs. Smyth introduced her husband, standing patiently by her side, cradling the tripod and smiling cordially.

"Nice to meet you, Thomas," Robert said, as he shook Mr. Smyth's hand. Robert turned back to Mrs. Smyth, asking, "You remember Angie, right?" Mrs. Smyth did, of course. Angie was her closest friend in school. "I ran into her last April. In Tokyo. Of all places! It's amazing how small the world is."

"Tokyo? What was Angela doing there?"

"She lives there, apparently. She's a product manager for Sony. Married a Jap. I ran across her at the

Tokyo airport. We didn't have a long chat. But it was amazing to see her after so long. And you too."

"Are you here with your wife?"

"No, no. Beth and I divorced years ago."

"Sorry."

"No worries. It's been a while." He paused to consider the complex passage of time. *Yes, it has been a while, hasn't it?*

Mr. Smyth was no longer standing attentively. His gaze wandered across the square in search of something else to film. Many of the building facades had immaculately restored frescos. Medieval scenes of muses in flowing gowns playing lutes and lyres. Women and girls dancing, holding wreaths and bouquets. Men leading oxen, quilling scrolls, balancing scales. An emperor sat upon an ornate throne. A heretic burned beneath a fiery stake.

"Would you like to join us for dinner a bit later?" asked Mrs. Smyth. "Are you here alone?"

Robert thanked her for the invitation, but declined. He already had plans. He was, at that very moment, hurrying to meet a young lady for lunch. They shook hands before parting, remarking on their good fortune for having met again so far from home.

The Smyths continued walking. They entered a busy shopping lane with windows displaying souvenir beer mugs and painted ceramics, expensive jewellery and watches, Bohemian crystal vases and decanters, memento keychains and t-shirts with beer slogans.

Two women, costumed in ornate Renaissance ball gowns, lured Mr. Smyth's attention. Their heads were adorned with excessive bundles of white nylon hair.

Their eyes hidden behind jewelled masks. They held flyers advertising a production of Mozart's *Marriage of Figaro* and assertively placed them into the hands of passing tourists.

Mr. Smyth held the camera to his shoulder. As he smoothed out the fur microphone cover and twisted the lens he said, "This right here is like traveling back in time."

Mrs. Smyth's feet hurt, but Mr. Smyth urged her onward. "The light is perfect now. I want to film the river once more. Afterwards we can go back to the room and rest before dinner." They waited on the sidewalk for a tram to pass. It cleared the tracks and Mr. Smyth darted into the street. Mrs. Smyth lingered, noticing another tram coming the opposite way.

There was no time to cry out. Rails screeched. Cars skid to a halt. Voices gasped. Mrs. Smyth was blocked in by the second tram and could not get across the street to view what had happened. Passengers aboard the tram seemed confused and irritated by the unexpected stop.

Mrs. Smyth hurried to the end of the tram and crossed the tracks. A crowd had gathered along the sidewalk. Numerous arms held cameras and phones all aimed in the same direction.

In the street, three men were crouched over a supine body. The body was alive, its eyes open, blinking. One man was speaking into his phone. Another leaned close to the injured man's face, listening. "His camera," said the man. "He wants his camera. Anybody?" Mrs. Smyth scrutinised the pavement. The video camera's many plastic parts and electronic entrails were strewn beside the tram and along the rails.

The accident extended their holiday. While Mr. Smyth recovered in Františku Hospital, having his body rehydrated and arm set properly, Mrs. Smyth rescheduled their flight, completed insurance papers, phoned her sister who was taking care of their cats, and checked into a hotel across the street from the hospital.

One evening, after visiting hours, Mrs. Smyth rode the tram across the river to view the cherry orchard along Petřín Hill. The guide book indicated they were well worth visiting that time of year.

It was an older tram, with orange fibreglass seats set atop inverted metal buckets. It smelled of musk and tobacco. As the tram turned toward Újezd Street, Petřín Hill rose into view. It ascended from beds of bright red roses. Beyond the flowers were darks slopes of grass, thickets of pine and some taller trees. The dense foliage ascended toward the Hunger Wall, which ran atop the hill. Further along were the fruitful pink cherry orchards Mrs. Smyth hoped to soon view.

As Mrs. Smyth strolled past the entrance to the funicular railcar and headed up the pathway, she approached a bronze statue of a handsome young man gazing at a bouquet of flowers, while absent-mindedly writing upon a sheet of parchment beside him. His name was carved in gold letters along the pedestal. *Karel Hynek Mácha.* Surrounding the statue were withering bouquets of wild flowers and flaming votive candles.

She consulted her guidebook. *Karel Hynek Mácha, poet (1810-1836). These people must love their poets,* Mrs. Smyth speculated. She sympathized. She had once dated a poet at University. The affair did not last long. She found him pretentious with a nonsensical grasp of reality. The shameless poems he had written her, though, were still kept somewhere among her old possessions.

Mrs. Smyth eventually halted her ascent. The looming pines and evergreens overshadowed the meandering pathways. She became disoriented and she could not tell which direction would lead her to the cherry orchard.

Hushed voices emerged from the dark beneath the foliage — whispers, foreign and unintelligible. Were they speaking to her? She could not tell from which direction they came. *Where were they? Who are they?* A chill rose up her spine. She turned and hurried back along the path.

At the bottom of the hill, a tram came to a stop at the platform. She hurried on board without checking the tram number and took a seat close to the door. Her heart clattered as the tram rode along the tracks. Outside her windows, beneath the glowing street lamps, she could not recognise a familiar building, storefront or any landmarks. Was she even headed in the right direction?

"Hold still," whispered a male voice behind her. Mrs. Smyth froze, afraid to turn.

"Like this?" a woman's hushed voice replied.

"There's more like it," said the man. "Relax yerself."

They both sounded familiar.

"What dee ya think? How's this now?"

"Orite."

Mrs. Smyth could no longer refrain from taking a glimpse. She turned. A young couple were sharing the same seat. The girl sat upon the young man's lap. They kissed, mouth covering mouth, oblivious to the world passing outside their window or the few other passengers aboard the tram.

Could they have been the couple from Bristol? The ones from the opposite side of the partition in that horrible pension where she and Mr. Smyth had been staying?

The young woman was slim and beautiful, just as Mrs. Smyth had imagined. Her arms were bare. Her legs covered in black nylon leggings with a small vertical rip on the thigh. One hand pressed against the young man's chest. The other extended between his legs. Mrs. Smyth wanted to turn away, but could not. She clutched her guide book so tight it sprung from her hands and onto the floor beneath the young man's legs. She cautiously leaned forward. The couple were too absorbed in their feral ardor to notice Mrs. Smyth's hand reach beneath them and retrieve the tousled guide book.

Mr. Smyth stirred the remaining gin and ice with his plastic swizzle stick. His opposite arm rested against his belly, ensconced in plaster. He signalled the flight attendant for another gin and tonic.

Mrs. Smyth had already warned him twice about drinking while on pain medication. He did not listen. And she did not need to continue going on about it. So she turned her attention to the P. D. James novel she had purchased at the airport book shop.

Mr. Smyth, awaiting his drink, shifted in his seat and stared out the window at the endless grid of sage and amber fields below. The camera's replaceable, he thought, but not the images it contained. A crushed memory card cannot be saved. The word *unrecoverable* kept repeating in his mind.

"What's that?" said Mrs. Smyth, setting aside her book. "Did you say something, Dear?"

Mr. Smyth wasn't aware he'd spoken out loud. "I was thinking about my movie," he said. "So many great moments. All gone. Just like that." He snapped his fingers.

"We have our memories."

"Of course. But that's not the same."

As they headed into the clouds, mist swept over the wings of the airplane. In no time, they would be landing at Stansted airport. They would take an Uber back to their flat in Tonbridge, where Mr. Smyth, with the assistance of Gordon's gin, would continue to mourn the loss of his home movies, while Mrs. Smyth, searching the dusty attic, would rediscover those worthless old poems mailed to her by an untoward, young poet many years before.

Fourth Notice

I am good at what I do, especially considering it is not something I have been formally trained in doing. I was once merely a clerical accountant, without even CPA accreditation. I did general accounting and admin. But when the laws regarding debt collection loosened to allow a more direct, vigilante approach, I was asked to try my hand at what we now euphemistically refer to as "Fourth Notice."

Dan Appleby, our Managing Director, dropped a stainless steel Remington with silencer on my desk. He said, "Can you manage one of these babies?" At the time, I never dreamt I could become an adept shooter. But it was either rise to the occasion or fall like the old guard, those who sank to the muddy bottom rather than flow with the changing times.

On payroll, I am still listed as Accountant, though it's been quite some time since I've actually kept books, crunched numbers or filed returns. My current position has more to do with right-ing bad debts. Around here, students with overdue payments receive three warning notices. They are urged to expediently settle accounts or make suitable arrangements with the Student Administration Finance Enforcement (SAFE) for future payments. There is no fourth warning document or written statement of any kind. There is only me.

Technically, what I do is *not* illegal. There are cable companies, mortgage firms, payday lenders, and even fresh water delivery services that employ people like myself to resolve bad debts in a similar manner. For most businesses, though, it's a PR nightmare. They tend to stick with the old methods. Continued harassment. Applying liens. Paycheck withholdings. Contracting, subcontracting and sub-subcontracting collection agencies until the arrears are so widely dispersed, they nearly vanish into the books.

The university where I work is otherwise discreet about fiscal matters. We do not have an official policy regarding bad debts. And they will never acknowledge my role in any of the disappearances. They fear students would otherwise retaliate. Protest. They do not want to incite the sort of water privatization riots that occurred in 2036. Damage to university property exceeded 13 million BMUs (Blockchain Monetary Units) that year. Nearly a quarter of the student body was necessarily gassed unconscious and kept manacled for 48 hours while medical teams administered Quaylinol to calm nerves and surgeons focused ultrasound radiation beams to dissolve recent memories.

I am not a violent person. I do not like blood. I like balance and order and columned ledgers. I like a well run home and fresh, clear water. I like schedules, routines and regular business hours. But we are living in different times. The world no longer functions as orderly as before. We are not as rule bound and regulated. The easy solutions have failed. People are now forced to attempt more radical approaches.

I know of some colleagues at SAFE who have secretly worked with black market pharmaceutical firms. Others who have fixed the books for commercial militia orgs, Russian Oligarchs and Nigerian Water Lords. Our former accounting EA was found to be moonlighting as one of the top five regional execs for the migrant slave trade. One could never tell any of this simply by their appearance. They each resembled typical clerks, auditors, statisticians and admins. They looked like friends and neighbors. Uncles and Aunts. Mother and fathers. Thin haired. Fat limbed. Diabetic. Ulcerated. Medicated on antidepressants, H2-receptor blockers and proton pump inhibitors. All just trying to survive, really.

There is an extensive protocol to Fourth Notices. It took several months before I was able to consistently meet each requisite involved in an "audit." No ties to the university must remain tethered. No witnesses. No signs of forced entry, blood-soaked carpeting or membrane-splattered walls.

During our first two years of Fourth Notice operations, I was solely responsible for making the bodies disappear without a trace. This is both easier and more difficult than it sounds. For one thing, it is never easy lugging an inert corpse down multiple flights of stairs or hefting one into the trunk of a car. But the actually *vanishing* is not hard. There are numerous small agencies specialising in this. Technically, your everyday mortuary can do the job, reduce a body quick to ash. But mortuaries are often run by people who — at least in my experience — are not wholly trustworthy. They will sometimes photograph and ID a corpse before incineration, then contact family members, selling off information about their deceased loved one's location and circumstances. Often, it's to subsidise their low wages. Or pay off their own student loans.

I no longer work alone. I have a team to assist me now — Serge, Cobain and Bret. They come and handle the bodies. They do the heavy lifting and make sure each debtor is swiftly transferred to the closest available drop-off point, while I move on to the next location, the next unsettled account.

At the end of my work day, which can sometimes be close to midnight, I complete a good hour's worth of paperwork. I note names, times, locations… I indicate whether it had been a clean kill or if any complications occurred. Witnesses, if any, would require specific notation. Personal affects catalogued. Expenses itemized. Etcetera. Pages upon pages of documentation must be completed before any debt is properly written off.

Earlier this evening, I tracked down a debtor at the Drifting Sands Motor Lodge off I-49. She had carelessly tried to reserve a room with a payment card associated with an overdrawn BMU account. An alert flashed on my mobile. I followed GPS coordinates to the motel and bribed the anorexic, feathered-hair receptionist in her "MY LIFEGUARD WALKS ON WATER" t-shirt for the room number.

Room 16 was along the backlot of the motel, facing a dried river basin. The parking lamps were at half power, radiating an orange glow along with an incessant, cicada-like drone. A navy blue P. T. Cruiser with Canadian plates was parked in front of the room next door.

I drove my Cherriola Ranchero toward the green metal trash dumpster at the edge of the lot and parked in its shadow. From my rearview mirror I had a direct vantage on Room 16. Shade curtains were drawn, but tungsten light filtered through them and onto the cement walkway. A black silhouette passed beyond the curtains. Clearly a woman's curved outline, coiffed hair, and swaying gait. I sipped slowly at my water flask while keeping an eye on the shapely figure pacing back and forth. After some time, the room darkened. I gave it another twenty minutes before making my move.

Blasting through locks with my Remy is rarely necessary. In cases like this, a gentle knock and soft-spoken explanation will often suffice. The trick for overcoming suspicion and distrust is simple and age-old: Money.

"Excuse me, Ms. Laromir?" I paused to listen through the door. "I'm sorry to bother you at this hour. Some fellow dropped off a cashier's check at Reception. Said you would be needing this." After a pause, I heard the bolt slide. I kicked. The door swung and the chain lock busted loose.

The woman stumbled backwards. "What is this?! Get out! Get out or I'll —" Her eyes locked onto my graduation cap — my *calling card* — worn to signal my purpose. She began to stammer. "Listen, I know why you're here, but it's a mistake."

"You know how many times I've heard that line, sister?" I moved the tassel left to right, as was my custom, before engaging the trigger.

"How many?" said a man's voice from behind me. I kept the gun aimed at the girl as I slowly turned toward the twin bed. "Tell me, Dick. How many times have you heard that line?"

It was an old man, lying beneath the sheets, a tank of oxygen on the blanket beside him and a plastic respiratory mask pulled atop of his grey-haired skull.

Despite the hollowed eyes and thinning hair, I recognized my old colleague, Gretch. He'd taken early retirement during the transition to Fourth Notices. I hadn't seen or heard from him since, though it was rumoured he had retired to a small cabin in Alberta.

"He has nothing to do with this," said the woman. "It's me you came for."

"Lucy, honey, I can handle this," said Gretch. "Listen, Dick. My condition is terminal. I asked Lucy to make me the loan's primary debtor, but she refused. You can simply swap our names. Terminate me and your job is done."

"It's not that simple, Gretch. You know that."

"I know nothing of the sort. You've been an accountant long enough to understand how things *really* work. Numbers only tell half the story. Not even that. Listen, I know where nearly every board member at the university keeps BMU accounts in escrow. That information has to be worth something to you."

The old man was bluffing, buying time. Lucy was gently sobbing, but I've heard such sobs before. You get used to it. Two bullets and my work here would be complete. Home to bed before sunrise, if I'm lucky.

"I'm sorry about this, Gretch. I'm only doing my —"

Before I could complete my exculpation, a blast shook the motel's foundation. Dentures submerged within Gretch's bedside glass rattled. The ceiling light flickered. A curtain drawstring swayed.

The blast was quickly followed by a thousand-finger tap-tapping against the window pane. Lucy pulled open the curtain. "Rain," she said. Light from the room reflected from each bead of water. Glistening rivulets fell like stars. I couldn't recall the last time I'd seen rain. Must have been in my twenties, back when I was still a student. They said it would never happen again.

"A miracle," whispered Gretch.

A gunshot resounded. A bullet roused the hairs upon my left ear as it whizzed past. I turned toward the old man. He was brandishing a rifle, drawn from beneath the bed sheet. The stupid, old fool. My reflexes were automatic. First shot knocked the oxygen mask off his head, piercing his skull. Second shot entered Lucy's breast, straight into those double-dealing champers of her insolvent heart.

I put in a call to my cleanup boys and got out of there lickety split. There was a long drive ahead. And complicated paperwork to complete.

The storm followed me as I headed East. I struggled to see through the rainy window. I'd driven quite far before I thought to use the wipers. I'd forgotten they were originally invented to clear rain off window glass, not just dust and sand.

The two mechanical arms smeared dirty water across the surface, eventually clearing a patch of visibility. Rain slashed through my headlight beams. Tires spat mud along the bottom-panels of my Ranchero. It seemed a waste, all that valuable fresh water going into the ground. If only we could store and track rainwater like bytes of currency. If only there were agents who would accrue, regulate, and proportion its distribution.

A long black limousine sped past, strewing precious sheets of water from beneath. Had it been Serge, Cobain and Bret, already on their way to the motel to disappear the bodies?

Within every small town I passed I saw people scurrying beneath street lamps. They carried buckets and hauled barrels, gathering the last drops of the diminishing rain-pour. Tomorrow, they will line up along roadsides with their containers, selling bags and bottles of rainwater to passing motorists. Same as I had done as a kid during those last days before the rains completely stopped.

Back at the office. 2 a.m. I'm not entirely sure how to fill out the paperwork on this one. I tack on an additional 3-80B report to disclose my personal association in the matter. I don't want any trouble from Dan Appleby, who might have questions about Gretch's involvement in this incident. I do not, however, mention the BMU escrow ruse Gretch proffered, which could only lead to an unnecessary and embarrassing Federal revue of the case, and place me in, if not hot water, certainly a less appreciated position with the board.

Is there shame in what I do? For sure. Few people actually enjoy killing. But we all make compromises for the sake of our employment. If I wasn't doing Fourth Notices, somebody else would. It's up to legislators and business leaders to determine what practices are just and necessary. Not me. I'm making a legal living, supporting a family as best I can. I do what the law abides.

You can look at it this way: debtors, like Lucy, will never overcome their circumstances. They will always be falling behind, forever struggling to keep head above quicksand. That's the kind of people they are — a continual burden on us all, accumulating greater and greater debt over the years, soaking up our limited resources, dwindling our fresh water reserves, burdening administrations with unnecessary paperwork and legal complexities. What I do, in a way, advances progress and keeps us all safe.

I make rationalisations, I know. But don't we all?

When I finally make it home, I will reheat the souf-flé Elfride, my wife, has likely prepared and set aside for me. After a quick bite, I will go upstairs to check the children, Evelyn and Gustav. I will peer through their bedroom door to observe my little wonders snug beneath blankets, peacefully asleep. Safe. Warm. Loved and watched over. At such moments, I ponder what kind of world they will inherit. A better one, I hope. One not burdened by so much debt and depletion. One where accountants, pharmacists, reservoir owners and bottlers need not bear arms. One with both sun and rain, wealth and security. I will kiss my darlings, each tenderly on the brow, then enter the washroom to complete my ablutions before preparing for bed. I will sleep well — I almost always do — knowing whatever compromises I have made with my life are worth it — if for no other reason than for the sake of the children.

Art of the Shave

Vic is not one bit nervous despite this being the night of his solo exhibition. He picks out a tea green vintage tuxedo shirt from his armoire. Throws on a yellow jacket, the one Yana brought him from Shanghai. He appraises himself in the door mirror. He is satisfied. *This will do*, Vic thinks. He appears competent yet casual, stylish without being trendy. The black stubble on his jaw is precisely managed. His neck shaved smooth. His ear...

Afternoon light from the window glistens off a long dark hair dangling from his right ear lobe. Vic goes to the bathroom, takes a tweezer from the medicine cabinet and examines his reflection in the sink mirror. He pinches the lobe with the tweezer until the serrated tips grip the errant hair. He pulls. The lobe distends, but the hair does not break free.

He tries a sharp, sudden yank. The tweezer flies from his hand. It bounces on mini-tiles in the shower stall and lands atop the drain.

Vic retrieves the tweezer and tries again. He searches for the hair. It has curled in upon itself, out of view behind the ear, as if hiding. He brushes it out with a fingertip, then surrounds it with the tweezer. The tweezer clamps down. He gives a tug. The whole ear moves side to side as he pulls in different angles. *This fucker is rooted deep*, he thinks. It would be easier to snip it off.

He keeps a pair of small scissors in a dresser drawer. He searches amidst the old phone chargers, dead batteries, dry felt markers and postcards, but does not find any scissors.

Vic interrupts his search to check the event page for the exhibition on his laptop. The event pages shows Yana has finally accepted his invite. He had hoped she would. And hoped she wouldn't. Now she did. What would she think? It didn't matter. He'd done his best work. Fuck it.

Vic continues to search for the scissors. He checks beneath the bedside table, inside the bamboo box where Yana kept her sewing supplies. Not there. Then he empties the shortbread tin in the armoire where he keeps his weed, tobacco and rolling papers. Not there, either. He thinks, *Maybe the kitchen? Possibly the utensil drawer?* That's where he finds them, alongside the butter knives, plastic ties, wine corks and a pair of decorated porcelain chopsticks.

He returns to the bathroom and once again locates the shiny, dark hair attached to the earlobe (*ear nipples*, Yana calls them). He draws thumb and fingertip down its length. Depending on the angle, it is nearly invisible within the mirror, tethered to the now pink and tender sack of adipose tissue.

The hair repeatedly slips out of his grip. It takes several tries before he gains a steady enough hold. Grasping the scissors with his left hand, he directs the lower blade toward the lobe. The scissors, however, will not cooperate. Every intended move turns into its opposite. It is like an optical illusion. He must make his hand do the reverse of what he is thinking. He keeps trying but it is no use. His mind won't cooperate. He is wasting time. Perhaps a razor would be best.

He removes the Art of the Shave Complete Wet Shave Kit from the medicine cabinet. It is a leather, zippered case with brush, oil, cream and stainless steel razor. Practically untouched. A gift from Yana on his thirtieth birthday. *Last thing she ever bought me*, he recalls.

"Look at the handle." She pointed out the engraving. It had his full name. "I never go by my full name," Vic responded. It was the wrong thing to say at the time, he knew.

In the mirror, his name appears backwards on the razor handle. The letters look foreign, almost Cyrillic. He holds the blade close to his ear. He shuts his eyes and works by touch alone. The razor glides against the skin. It is a gentle, smooth motion. Somehow, though, the blade removes flesh. Blood flows from an imperceptible wound. It splats down his neck and onto his yellow jacket collar, leaving a sanguine spot the size of a dime.

He removes the jacket and places the collar beneath cold running water. His ear drips blood into the sink, while Vic brushes the collar with a bar of liquorice body soap. The stain lifts into the pinkening foam. He rinses the collar again and hangs the jacket upside down over the door to dry.

Returning to the mirror, he examines the wound. A drop of blood dangles from the tip of his ear. A crimson line runs along the side of his neck toward his chest. It looks like he has been in a knife fight, not simply nicked by a shaving razor. The splatter of blood makes him woozy. The bathroom lighting brightens and expands in circumference, like a projector burning through strip of celluloid film.

He is not sure how much time has passed, or why he is lying on the bathroom tile. His jaw is clenched. There is a sharp pain at the center of his forehead. He turns on his side. A circle of blood, no larger than a drain stop, is darkening upon the white tile. He remembers his ear, the bleeding. He rises to his feet, peers into the mirror. His jaw is yellow, his eyes swollen. Blood has coagulated along the edge of his right ear. There's a faint ringing noise in his head. More like a high-pitched drone, really. Possibly, his phone, he thinks.

He removes the phone from his pant pocket. "Hello?"

Vic hears nothing. He switches to the opposite ear. "Hello," he says again. "I can't hear you. Something's wrong with my phone."

The missed call reads *unknown*. He checks the time. He is running late. He has less than an hour to get to the gallery, but the damn yellow jacket is still wet at the collar.

He plugs in the blow dryer. There is no sound, but he feels its heat. The hairs upon his wrist bend and quiver. He realises his hearing is gone. *This is just temporary*, Vic assures himself. *These things happen. Don't they? A hard blow to the jaw can do that. Right?*

Vic presses the nozzle into the material to expedite the drying process. He recalls the time he first received this jacket from Yana. It had been a peace offering, of sorts, upon her return from China. They had fought shortly before she'd left to start her residency in Shanghai. She had loved it and wanted to return.

"I could probably go again, work on something larger," she had said. "Wouldn't you like to live with me in China for a couple years?"

The idea was absurd to Vic. He had no money to relocate and would never risk losing his cheap rental studio at the old wallpaper factory.

"Forget about money," she'd said. "If money weren't an issue, would you? Would you be willing to leave everything behind and go with me?"

Her return to Shanghai the following summer drove them apart. But it also drove him to create. He completely reworked old canvases. Participated in group shows at the factory complex. Experimented with new media. People began to take notice. He was invited to exhibit in other parts of town. His social calendar filled up. He partied a lot. Slept with his students at the art institute. Stayed out all night. Tried Oxycodone and Dilaudid. Would lay in bed past noon. Unbound. Completely free. It showed in his work. Powerful brush strokes. Grotesque figures in iridescent hues. Raw energy. It was undeniable. Everyone saw it. She would, too, if she had the courage to admit it. Could she even bear to look? Would she weep with regret, plead for forgiveness? No. Not Yana. Her pride would not allow it. He would get a polite "congratulations" and that's all.

The scent of burning synthetics returns Vic's attention to the hand dryer. He switches off the blower and examines the jacket collar. The dryer's heat has left a faint discoloration. *Though, hardly noticeable from a distance*, he thinks.

Vic slips his arms through the sleeves, then opens the medicine cabinet to remove a bottle of cologne — CK Eternity for Men — also a gift from Yana. *Earternity*, he jokes to himself. *Ha. Ha. Ha.* He sprays his wrists and neck. It smells of metal fence posts and rainstorms.

He checks his reflection in the mirror once more. His is shaken. He cannot believe what he sees. He'd been so distracted, disoriented, he'd forgotten about it. *You bastard*, he says to the hair, clinging definitely to his right ear. *What are you still doing there?*

He searches for the razor. "I will fuck you up," he says out loud, though his voice feels somewhat inaudible, coming not from his mouth, but somewhere deep inside his head "I will fuck you up good," he continues. "I will van Gogh my ear if I have to. Whatever it takes to rid myself of you."

Otherness

She stole away my best disappointments and worries. I tried to get them back, tried to find where she hid them, but she wasn't telling. "You don't need those any more," Janine said. "But I do," I insisted. "I've had them for so long. They're comfortable." "You don't need them any more," she repeated. "You can always get new ones, Drew. Those were too old and skanky to keep around."

So I got on with things, learned to live without my disappointments and worries. At first, it seemed like bad taste walking around without them, like wearing Kelly green chinos on a snowy day. I thought people were staring at me. Maybe they were. But for once I wasn't worried about it.

I realized there were *others*. You don't normally meet them when you're walking around, stooped over, burdened by a half-dozen worries bearing down on you. But apparently they've always been there, going about their lives without a care in the world.

I met Alice in a wine bar in my neighborhood. I had gone there to sit and skim through a book on Tibetan culture that I'd stumbled across. Alice and I struck up a conversation over the book. She was a Tibetophile, or whatever you call them. She'd been to Lhasa, the holy city. She intended to stay one week, but the snows came early and stranded her. While waiting for the spring thaw, Alice studied Buddhist Meditation and learned to levitate three feet off the ground. "The body is heavy, but the soul is light," she said. "I can't seem to float like that any more, though. There are too many distractions in city life. But that's a mindful trade-off I've made in order to be more connected to this world."

Frank was this tall, strapping fellow who worked the meat counter at QuickShop. I'd been buying ground beef and poultry there for years. Up until this time, we'd never exchanged more than the usual *What can I getcha?* and *Make it a pound and a quarter*. Frank had long dark sideburns extending from his lower jaw all the way up to his white paper cap. His shoulders ran at perfect 90 degree angles from his neck. He stood so straight, he appeared as if pinned against an invisible wall. For some reason — and I can't even remember how it started — Frank and I got into a conversation about transcendental phenomenology. He'd been reading Husserl, he said. "Take this ground chuck. What is it really? I don't know. Neither do you. All we know is our experience, right? I'm not really selling meat. I'm selling the experience of meat." I walked away with three pounds of natural prime ground chuck wrapped in butcher paper, thinking what a shame it had taken so many years for us to strike up a conversation.

I met Leslie that same week. She was a painter, attending the Japanese calligraphy class I was also enrolled in. It was her second time taking the class, she said. She couldn't get enough of it. *Let the monkey mind go and the squid ink flow.* Leslie drove a brand new Harley Davidson, custom painted reddish-pink, like the color of freshly spanked skin. She often gave me rides home.

One day, we stopped at her studio so she could show me her work. The paintings were large. Maybe six by eight feet. They contained a lot of white space surrounding a variety of circular orbs. "They look like you could climb inside them," I said. "You think so?" She was pleased by this response. "And what would you do if you climbed inside?" "I'd try to figure out where all those orbs were coming from."

It wasn't long before I found myself having an affair with Leslie. And then one with Alice. And, with Frank and I — that was as inevitable as cigarettes after coffee. Of course, I kept none of this from Janine. Why should I? She was the one who made it possible for me to meet people like Alice, Leslie and Frank. I had her to thank for this freedom. And — I made it clear — it was her companionship I valued most of all.

For her 28th birthday, I treated Janine to a lavish surf and turf dinner at The Park, toasted her with champagne and paid for a carriage ride through the slushy streets of the city center. It was all going splendidly until I mentioned Leslie was having a dinner party the following Saturday and that Leslie was looking forward to finally meeting Janine.

"Will Alice and Frank be there?" Janine asked. "Most likely," I said. "We're all becoming quite good friends." "I'd call it more than friends," Janine said, with perhaps a bit of sarcasm in her voice. "Is there a problem here?" I asked. "Of course not," she said. She quietly dropped the subject. I figured everything was okay and she would come Saturday to see what great people they all were and be fine with everything.

But Saturday came and Janine refused to get ready for the party. "I don't feel like going," she said. "Everyone is looking forward to meeting you," I replied. But it was no use. She wanted to stay in and that was that. She told me to go ahead without her.

I went. It was a good party. Leslie made bouillabaisse with these strange purple and red tentacles that come from a certain squid that exists only off the northeastern coast of Newfoundland. There were twelve dinner guests in all. Each was fun and interesting, contributing equally to the conversation, which for some reason mostly revolved around intellectual property rights, cures for sinusitis, Canadian hockey and real estate.

After the other guests departed, Alice, Frank, Leslie and I relaxed on the sofa, wrapping our boundless limbs around one another, sharing a joint and talking about renting a cabin in the mountains, so we could all be together on New Year's Eve, as the new millennium arrives.

Frank asked if he could bring someone. "Who?" asked Alice. Frank explained he'd started seeing a girl, Sharon, with whom he'd gotten quite close. "Sharon Waznicky?" asked Alice. "I can't believe it. I thought you two were completely over."

"You should bring her," said Leslie. "Drew is going to bring Janine, right?"

"Of course," I said.

"Well, then I'm going to invite a couple of men to balance things out," said Alice.

"That's okay with me," said Frank.

"Really?" said Alice.

"Sure," said Frank.

"We should all bring whomever we want," said Leslie.

Of course, we all agreed.

Daylight had begun creeping through the alleys between buildings by the time I got home. I entered the apartment and quietly removed my coat and Timberlands. Janine was not in the bedroom. She was not in the kitchen or the living room or the office, either. Her boots and winter coat, however, were still in the hallway by the front door. *There's nothing to worry about*, I thought. I brushed my teeth and prepared for bed.

Before turning off kitchen lights, I took a quick look at the enclosed back porch. That's where I found Janine. She was lying upon the un-insulated floorboards, nestled in a pile of my old worries and disappointments, her body curled within their twisted folds. I thought those old worries and disappointments had been tossed out, gone forever. Apparently they'd been stashed out of sight, deep within some crawl space above the ceiling or below in the cellar storage unit, maybe.

Janine was almost entirely covered in this jumble of old concerns and notions. Only the top of her head and one bare shoulder stuck out. There was a lot of them, more worries and disappointments than I remembered ever having. It took a few moments before I realized some were hers, also, her own worries and disappointments. And others were some we had shared.

I entered the porch and got on my knees. Janine's eyelids parted. Her sleepy eyes peered at me. Even in the dusty sheen of first light, I saw the skin surrounding her lids was swollen and pink as a pork chop. Those many worries and disappointments seemed to frame and accentuate her features in a way that cleaved deep into my heart, making Janine more beautiful than anything I had ever imagined or seen. She gave a weak smile, lips quivering at their corners. I leaned forward, lifted some of those old worries and disappointments and crawled in beside her.

Life Raft

Despite the troubled waters and the threat of sharks, everyone aboard the rubber raft kept their manners. The ill discreetly heaved overboard, wiped, apologized. The men offered jackets and scarfs to the shivering ladies. Those with pocketed snacks — candy bars, mints, crackers, nuts — politely shared with all. Nearly everyone kept good cheer and tried to ease any fears. *We'll be found in no time!...Quite an adventure we're having!...Chin up!*

They were wet at the seat of their trousers, along the trim of their wraps and gowns. Shoes and stockings clung cold and heavy to their shrivelled toes. Lips puckered with salt. Hair stiffened from sea spray and wind. *Think positive*, they told themselves. And each other. They were alive, after all. *Look forward to the next warm shower...bath salts...wax candles...trees... flowers... fresh mowed grass...the embrace of small children...sizzling Porterhouse steaks...long, cozy naps beneath warm, dry blankets...*

"Does anyone have a cigarette?" asked the gentleman with the blue ascot and large, opal cufflinks. A few passengers searched their pockets. "All wet, mine are," said the curly-haired violinist. A lady in a pink flared dress, blood splatter across the open back, retrieved a pack of Davidoffs from her white purse.

"I have half a pack, if anyone is in need." She handed her pack to the man with the blue ascot who thanked her as he removed a cigarette and passed the pack to another gentleman who wore a ruffled tuxedo shirt, tails flapping in the breeze. They shared a pocket lighter. The timorous women with the burgundy headscarf jotted notes or, perhaps, calculations in her plastic, yellow binder. Someone shouted, "Look, an eagle!" They peered up at the sky. It was not an eagle, but some other large bird, perhaps a goose making a solo journey home across the sea.

The sunset was beautiful, they agreed. The water slowed to a gentle chop. The sun merged into the gilded horizon like butter melting into syrup. The air began to brisken. "Keep close, everyone. It's going to be a long night. We've enough warmth here for all." It was Hogarth who said that, the gentleman who had sadly lost his petite French bulldog. The advice was hardly necessary. They were already situated shoulder to shoulder within the small raft.

Fernando the violin player spoke at a whisper to Marrialle beside him. "Do you mind if I wrap an arm around you, Miss?"

"Not at all. Please."

Two ladies wearing matching taffeta gowns clung to Marko — the man was practically a giant and his immense body generated great heat.

"Aren't we quite the crew," spoke the man with the

ascot, whom the others referred to as Mr. Frost. Everyone laughed. "We will have a real story to tell our grandchildren." They all agreed.

The raft flowed with the current. Days passed. Then weeks. Eventually, Marrialle announced she was pregnant. Everyone congratulated her and Fernando. All insisted they marry aboard the raft. Mr. Merryweather could officiate. Mr. Frost, spying some large fish leaping distantly off starboard side, announced they would have a great feast that evening to celebrate — *if only Marko got busy and managed to snare one of those large porpoises.*

Everyone made an effort to snatch what they could from the sea. There were tiny squids. Small whistle back minnows. Sea hedgehogs. Red anemones that Mr. Frost called Chinese Lanterns. And a package of salted pork that Simone spotted afloat a short distance from the raft.

"The expiration date is still good," she exclaimed.

"Wouldn't risk it," said Hogarth.

"Let me see that." Mr. Frost took the package and examined the label. "It's fine," he said. "These things will remain edible long after we're all expired."

"We need to do something nice about your hair," said Louise Broom to Marrialle.

"Oh, it's fine," said Marrialle. But Louise Broom insisted.

Mr. Merryweather searched his prayer book for a suitable passage to read aloud. Marko sharpened his carving stiletto upon the anchor blade. The rest, under Mrs. Merryweather's instruction, practiced their singing voices. They repeated their 'Do-Re-Mi's and 'Fa La La's over and over causing the gulls circling above to join in with joyful calls of their own.

With a veil of crinoline shading Marrialle's chocolate brown eyes, and Fernando's shirt and jacket patched and sewn, the couple were finally ready. They knelt upon nearly dry, orange fire-blankets. Mr. Merryweather licked a finger and flipped through the playing-card size pages of his prayer book. With trembling hands, he held the text close to his one good eye.

"Love never fails," he read, his voice quivering slightly with emotion and, perhaps, ailment. "Where there are prophecies, they will cease; where there are tongues, they will be stilled; where there is knowledge, it will pass away. But love, my dear ones — love never fails."

The happy couple enthusiastically kissed with tongues like writhing eels within toothsome wreaths of white coral. Everyone shouted, *Hurray!* and offered congratulations. Even Violette, who normally preferred to commit her thoughts solely to the yellow binder rather than speak out loud, warmly commended the couple.

After the ceremony, the passengers sang popular songs. "Tie a Yellow Ribbon." "Sealed With a Kiss." "(I Never Promised You a) Rose Garden." They passed canteens of rainwater. They relished the porpoise Marko flayed and grilled in the metal tire rim tethered behind the raft by rope and wire.

"What I wouldn't give for a cigarette," sighed Simone as she gnawed upon a salty mackerel fin.

Louise Broom, gleefully asserted that her bottle caps of rainwater were actually vodka shots. Marko played percussion on his chest, biceps, jowls and massive forehead. Simone removed her brassiere from beneath her sleeveless gown and spun it like a propeller.

"You people are too much," laughed Fernando.

"What are you going to name the baby?" asked Mrs. Merryweather.

"Bottiglioni," replied Fernando.

Everyone cheered.

Marrialle laughed and squeezed Fernando's arm. "Seriously, though," she said, "he'll be named Roberto."

"Yes, that's fine," agreed Fernando.

Often, the sea toyed with them. Larger waves sometimes buckled the raft's rubber underbelly as if trying to unseat its passengers. Other times, smooth, steady waves carried them like a conveyor belt.

A single wave once bore them high, hefting the raft along as if transporting its passengers to their next location.

The giant wave took them past a chain of small tropical islands. "Such white sands," said Mr. Merryweather. "Such tall and leafy palms," added Simone. "Such a dream to behold," mused Louise Broom, as the last, tiny island faded into the mist.

Baby Robert (Bobby, as he was called), upon turning a year old, could sit, stand and crawl from lap to lap. Space became more constrained than ever. They economized as best they could. Only the most useful items were kept aboard. Additional supplies were pulled behind upon a regatta of plastic bottles and polyethylene tarp. Their archipelago of surplus goods consisted mainly of rainwater barrels, tubs of condensation, strips of dried kelp and cases of canned beans they had salvaged from a slowly sinking cargo container they'd come across.

They joked about what they would do once Simone's baby was born. Simone was three months into her own pregnancy, yet no one was quite sure who the father might be.

"One of us will need to make way for Simone's baby," said Marko. "I nominate Mr. Frost for he's the oldest." Everyone laughed knowing Marko was only joking. They could scarcely do without Mr. Frost with his prudent leadership and sage advice.

"We'd all fit fine if you'd just lose a little weight, Marko," chided Mr. Frost.

They agreed *not* to give presents that Christmas. The year before had been a struggle to salvage any refuse from the sea worth bestowing. In the end, half of what had been collected as gifts was thrown back overboard due to lack of space.

"If we're not gift giving this year," said Louise Broom, "we should still do something to celebrate."

So, that Christmas, they decorated the raft with ornaments from the sea. Purple urchins. Magenta beadlet anemones. Oxide crab shells. Green nuggets of sea-polished glass. Maroon and gold fire coral. Rainbow-hued cephalopods and bivalves. They filled conch shells with seal fat and the wax esters of shellfish, creating candles with smokey flames that whirled toward the stars. They danced, each taking his or her turn in the center of the raft. Waves rippled beneath them. Marko wet himself laughing. "Here's to the best Christmas ever," he toasted.

"Do fish sleep?"

Simone's child, Isabel, awaited an answer. She was seated on the edge of the raft, her minnow-sized toes flicking water. She had recently celebrated her fourth birthday and was considered by all an excellent swimmer.

"Heavens no!" said Hogarth. "Could you imagine? What would happen if you were swimming under water and fell asleep?"

"I'd be *drownded*," said Isabel.

"Exactly," said Hogarth.

"Stop it," said Simone.

"Stop what?"

"Stop talking about drowning. Yes, Isabel. Of course, fish sleep." She pulled Isabel onto her lap, away from Hogarth's cajoling. Isabel examined her mother's face, saw her mother was telling the truth and became quite sad imagining all those drowned fish.

During heavy storms, the passengers threw sheets of sail-cloth overhead. The rattling canvas was nearly deafening. "Hold tight," was Mr. Frost's famous cry. Those close to Marko clung to his giant limbs. The children, Bobby and Isabel, crouched low at the feet of the adults, their small bodies partially submerged in the roiling water aboard.

"It's like a roller coaster, isn't it?" This was Mrs. Merryweather's favourite expression. Large swells would often leave everyone queasy. Marrialle's stomach was particularly sensitive. Fernando would hold her by the waist as she leaned overboard. His lips pressed to the nape of her neck. "It's all good," he would whisper, his fingers combing back the wet curls.

In milder weather the children often swam beside the raft, exercising their small limbs and allowing a brief repose for the adults aboard. There were eventually three children. Marrialle and Fernando had a second boy. They named him Etienne, after the town where Marrialle was from. While Bobby and Isabel swam laps, circling the raft, Fernando would hold Etienne over the side, allowing him to practice his strokes and kicks. The others kept an eye out for jellyfish, sharks and anything else that might snap up a small child.

One day an albatross appeared on the cooking tire, its red feet splayed upon the charred metal. It was the first bird they'd seen in weeks. Marko crouched low, reaching for his spear. Simone held his arm back.

"Please, Marko."

"But we'll soon be hungry."

It was true. They hadn't caught anything but boney flying fish for days and found almost no edible package goods afloat. Plus, Mr. Frost temporarily forbade eating more kelp, for fear of surplus arsenic accumulating in the bloodstream.

"He's so beautiful," said Louise Broom, observing the bird. Its feathers were whiter than the whitest clouds, its beak a peachy yellow. Its honey-colored eyes, set within dark triangles, expressed an intelligence that seemed to comprehend their human thoughts.

"Bird! Bird!" shouted Etienne, waking from his nap.

"Hello, Mr. Seagull," said Simone. She held out a bit of dried sausage in her palm.

"That's good sausage," protested Hogarth. He quickly conceded. "Oh, okay. Let him have it."

Simone pulled herself forward. She steadied her body with one hand on Marko's shoulder, while extending the other hand toward the bird. The albatross stared at her face, then at the sausage, then back at her face. It leapt from its perch, seized the small bit of meat with its bill and flew away.

"There he goes," said Louise Broom as the bird soared toward the clouds. "He's sure to bring us good fortune."

Violette reached beneath her for the yellow binder and quickly jotted something down.

Mrs. Merryweather insisted the children receive a proper education. "You don't want them to grow up savages," she half-jokingly told Marrialle. The passengers all agreed to help, offering to teach whatever knowledge and skills they possessed.

"I can teach corporate taxation and insurance risk," stated Mr. Frost to everyone's amusement. In truth, Mr. Frost had wide-ranging knowledge. He had been a trustee for a large university before retirement. Among the many things he'd taught them were how to produce calcium carbonate and sulphites by boiling sea water, how to predict the weather by observing various cloud formations and how to carve sea creatures from driftwood and sea gourds.

Fernando, who had managed to restring his violin with nylon fishing line, offered to teach music. He tested the strings, plucking a simple melody, but it kept falling out of tune. Parts of the violin's lining had wood rot. The neck could not hold entirely straight. Fernando was determined, though. "I swear I will get her to play!"

Hogarth knew a thing or two about magic, he proclaimed. He produced playing cards he had secreted some place dry upon his body. Mrs. Merryweather disapprovingly furrowed her brows.

"Kids love magic," Hogarth insisted. "Watch, I'll make Mrs. Merryweather disappear into thin air." He raised his arms. Mrs. Merryweather, alarmed, lost balance trying to avoid Hogarth's spell and might have toppled overboard had Mr. Merryweather not taken hold of both her arms.

"A little fun and games is fine," said Mr. Frost, glancing over at Violette and her yellow binder. "But let's make sure they learn the basics first. Reading. Writing — "

"Cribbage and Canasta," quickly added Louise Broom, seizing the deck of cards from Hogarth's hand.

Isabel was restless and asked to swim before dark. She and Bobby circled the raft and leapt like dolphins. An occasional splash arced over the adults aboard the raft.

"For crying out loud," Hogarth said, wiping the sting of salt from his eyes.

Etienne stayed aboard due to an open wound on his right forearm. Earlier that day he'd cut himself bending a piece of tin into what he claimed was a periscope. The adults insisted he not go in. "Sharks, you know," said Louise Bloom flaring her nostrils as if she were a shark catching scent. "Oh, I'm not afraid of sharks," said Etienne.

The sky deepened from azure to Egyptian blue. They recognized the evening cloud formations from Mr. Frost's meteorology lessons. *Altocumulus castellanus,* was what Mr. Frost had called those small, vertical towers resting atop dark, wooly cloud mass. Also known as *celestial castles.*

Bobby and Isabel bobbed amongst the floating sea creatures carved earlier that day from sea gourds, laughing and squirting water from their mouths.

"How time flies," mused Simone. "Seems only yesterday the children were first learning to swim."

"They were just babies. Look at them now," said Mrs. Merryweather. Etienne made a face, protending his periwinkle stained tongue. Marrialle forced an arm around the child and rocked him as if he were still her baby boy.

"You people never cease to amaze me," said Violette. The others turned in her direction. They were surprised to hear the normally reticent Violette speak up. She added nothing more, however, and resumed writing copious notes in her yellow binder.

As the sun sank into cloud castle turrets, the youths climbed back aboard. They were still full of high spirits from their evening swim and Mr. Frost sought to calm them, as he frequently did, by telling stories, often of his wartime adventures in the Pacific.

"Have I told this already?"

"No," they lied, encouraging him to go on. Each telling was often an improvement on the last, revealing new details, anecdotes and characters.

"Once we were on a small island south of Panay. There were these enormous crabs. I'm telling you, twice the size of Marko's head. We would wrap them in banana leaves and bury them in a pit of burning embers to cook. Never tasted anything so delicious."

"What about the snakes?" said Isabel, squirming with delight.

"The snakes? You mean the anaconda? How did you know about those? Well, let me tell you —"

It was not always Mr. Frost who did the story-telling. Hogarth raised a few eyebrows with his tall tales of life on a haunted Indonesian fruit plantation. Fernando's accounts of revelries with fellow musicians could make the ladies blush right through their deep tans. Mrs. Merryweather fascinated all with her incredible mind for historic detail. Mr. Merryweather recollected passages from the Old and New Testament. Marrialle told fairy tales from her childhood in the French mountains. Simone dispassionately described her two fated marriages, first to a corrupt genealogist, then a ruthless antiques smuggler. Marko gave impersonations of his many colourful travel companions from the past with animated hand gestures and funny accents. And Louise Broom surprised all by divulging youthful indiscretions, the sort not normally mentioned in mixed company. Their stories fuelled many evening hours with an endless supply of diversion.

Mr. Frost, his voice growing hoarse, concluded his tale of the giant anaconda and the discovery of the island's secret burial vault with his usual ending: "And that, my friends, is a story for next time."

Louise Broom, Marko and then Hogarth also added their voices to the evening's storytelling session. Normally, they would all be tucked beneath tarp and sailcloth by that late hour, ready for sleep. But this particular night was different. An enormous super-moon hovered above the horizon making the wave caps magically glitter. Perhaps the moon, with its immense gravitational power, galvanized their imaginations, drawing forth narratives like a tide toward shore, a force so strong not even Violette could resist.

"I have one," said Violette.

The other passengers fell silent.

Violette continued. "I used to visit a group of seniors at their care center. They would sit together in a cramped living space. Without much else to occupy their time, they simply conversed, played silly games, sang old songs. They were like children. Always playing and pretending.

"When I last visited, I found them dressed in their fancies, a few wearing sunglasses. 'Shades,' they called them. They were going on a sea cruise, they said. 'Come with us.' 'I can't,' I tried to explain. 'It sounds wonderful, but I haven't the time.' 'Too late!' They all laughed. 'What's so funny?' I asked. 'We've already set off,' they said. 'Take your seat.' So I sat in one of the rocking chairs and right away they were chatting about the waves and the sea and the exotic places they hoped to discover. Someone broke out a bottle of sherry. One fellow produced a fiddle and began playing Italian mazurkas. We all stared out the bay window, rocking in our chairs, watching what looked like harbor lights twinkle and recede into the distance."

As Violette closed the yellow binder and slid it beneath her seat, a satisfied smile spread across her thin, chapped lips.

"How strange," said Louise Broom.

"I should like to meet such wonderful people," responded Marrialle.

"Yes," agreed Mr Frost. "Wouldn't we all?"

MULTIPLE CHOICE

The Precious Ball

Once there was a lonely girl whose only friend was a rubber ball. Whenever the girl and the ball went outside to play, she bounced the ball, threw it in the air and caught it as it came back down. One day, however, she was playing too close to a well. She threw the ball up and if fell out of reach, landing within the well. She looked for the ball, but the well was very deep and she could not see the bottom. She began to cry. She cried so hard her tears filled the well. The water rose higher and higher until the ball appeared, floating on the water's surface. She reached for it and...

A) Took the ball home, swearing she would never again play so close to a well.

B) Fell into the water and drowned.

C) Waited for her arm to grow.

D) Realized, deep down, balls make terrible friends and will always break your heart.

The Chipmunk & the Grasshopper

The chipmunk was busy gathering nuts and storing them away for the long, cold winter. He observed the grasshopper lazing about, playing music all day. "Grasshopper, if you don't start gathering food soon, you'll perish of hunger during the long, dark winter." Every time he said this, the grasshopper replied, "There is always time for a little music!" and went right on playing his fiddle. When the weather finally turned cold…

A) The chipmunk, surrounded by all his nuts, anticipated the joy he would feel turning away the hungry grasshopper.

B) The chipmunk became sick of nuts. *Nuts for breakfast! Nuts for lunch! Nuts for dinner!* He was so bloody sick of nuts, he set out in the frigid cold to find a grasshopper to eat.

C) The grasshopper was discovered by a talent agent from *Prairie's Got Talent*, became a television superstar and started dating Scarlett Johansson.

D) The grasshopper died during the first frost, completing his natural lifespan.

Lonely Hans

Lonely Hans was out wandering the forest when he came upon a deer caught in a trap. "Please help me," said the deer. Hans could not stand to watch an animal suffer, so he freed the deer.

The deer turned out to be an enchanted beast. "In return for saving my life, good sir, I will grant whatever wish you desire." Lonely Hans had simple needs and only asked for a home. "Your wish is granted," said the deer.

There, before Hans's very eyes, appeared no ordinary home. It was a majestic castle with splendid gardens and hunting grounds. "There is one catch," said the deer. "No one must ever enter the locked door within the tower."

A) Lonely Hans lived all his life, alone, in the castle. In old age, unable to bear his loneliness any longer, he jumped from the castle tower. As he fell through the air, it occurred to him there might be something worth living for behind that locked door.

B) Lonely Hans married. He was married a short time, though it felt much longer than it really was. One day his wife asked, "What is it you keep behind that locked door?" Lonely Hans replied, "Nothing to worry about. Let's not talk about it."

C) Lonely Hans had a daughter. One day she discovered a hidden key in the tower. Despite warnings from her father, she could not resist the temptation to open the locked tower door. The brass key turned, unlocked the door and it swung open. Inside she discovered the dead bodies of her grandparents, the king and queen, who had been trapped inside.

D) One day Lonely Hans heard music coming from behind the locked door. It sounded familiar, like something he had once heard on *Prairie's Got Talent*.

Beautiful Barbara

Even from a far distance, the young prince could see the girl in the high tower was a great beauty. Her skin glowed white as the moon and her long, flaxen hair flowed the entire length of the tower. He trotted closer to get a better look but by the time he reached the castle she was gone. He waited in vain all day and night for the girl to reappear in the window.

The next morning, an old witch approached the tower. The witch called out, "Barbara! Barbara! Let down your long hair!" The girl appeared in the tower window and let down her long, flowing hair. The witch climbed the hair and entered the tower window.

After the witch left, the prince came out of hiding. He stood beneath the window and called out, "Barbara! Barbara! Let down your long hair!" Cascades of beautiful, flowing hair descended upon him. He climbed until reaching the tower window.

A girl of truly great beauty greeted the young prince. I mean, like, *wow*. They soon became lovers. From then on, the young prince stealthily climbed Barbara's hair every evening to have a quickie.

One day, however, the witch made an unscheduled return to the tower. She arrived just in time to catch the young prince leap from Barbara's hair and set off on horseback. The witch was so enraged by this deception, she shaved every hair off the girl's pretty head.

After that…

A) The girl was able to use the discarded hair to form a parachute and soon escaped from her prison tower.

B)   The prince returned. And, as usual, he climbed
the hair. Only this time he was greeted by the
witch, holding the hair in her gnarly fingers.
Things did not go well for the prince after that,
to say the least.

C)   The prince cried out, "Barbara! Barbara! Let
down your long hair!" but there was no response. He kept crying out her name, but she did
not reply, thus confirming everything the prince
believed about the cruelty of pretty girls.

D)   After not receiving any response from the tower
window, the prince mounted his horse and rode
to the next tower a little further down the road,
where an even prettier girl was held captive.

Heinrich & Gretchen

The poor woodcutter and his wife could not find
enough food to feed their family. "Four mouths are too
many," insisted his wife. "We must rid ourselves of the
children in order to survive."

The woodcutter did not want to give up his children, but you can't argue with logic. So one day he
brought Heinrich & Gretchen deep into the forest. He
sent them to gather branches. When they returned, their
father was gone. They were lost, hungry and afraid.
They wandered ever deeper into the forest, until coming upon a house made entirely of sweets.

A)   They began to nibble at the house. Soon their
hunger vanished, but they were dying of thirst.

B)   Inside the witch was stewing with rage. Someone
was eating her house! She complained to her cat

and her owl and her clock and the fire in the hearth. *Children these days are so rude and impudent. Nobody teaches them manners!* But all that complaining got her nowhere.

C) The witch invited the children inside. Being a lonely witch, she greatly enjoyed their company. She served the children tea and told them about her life. She had done many things and traveled many places. Heinrich and Gretchen could not believe a person could talk so much. She went on and on, and would not shut up. Finally, the children interrupted. "We're sorry, but we have to be going now."

D) Heinrich and Gretchen ventured into the house. Inside they found the most beautiful girl they'd ever seen, with a shaved head, cowering in the corner.

The Shoemaker & the Devil

If the shoemaker had known how expensive it was to be married, he might have remained single. But as things were, he had many debts to pay and could not possibly make enough shoes to cover his wife's expensive shopping habits.

One day the Devil, dressed as a stylish nobleman, entered the shop. He greatly admired the shoemaker's work and proposed a joint partnership. His magic would double the shoemaker's productivity and greatly increase the shoemaker's wealth. In return, the Devil asked for only 15% of all profits.

In his excitement, the shoemaker signed the Devil's contract without reading the fine print. But, weeks later, he discovered a clause obliging him to hand over his second child.

"That's okay," said the shoemaker's wife. "We'll only have one child."

After their first child was born, the Devil returned to claim his due.

A) "You've made a mistake," said the shoemaker. "See here, the contract reads *second child*." "That's a one!" shouted the Devil. "It looks like a two," said the shoemaker. "That's definitely a two," agreed the shoemaker's wife. "That's ridiculous," said the Devil. "Why would I write two instead of one?" "You'll have to take that up with our lawyer," said the wife, putting an end to the discussion.

B) The Devil said, "I've come for your second child." He explained to the shoemaker that life begins at conception. Thus, an earlier miscarriage counted as the couple's first child. The shoemaker and his wife disagreed with this definition of life. They fell into a huge argument, which still rages on to this very day, despite the child now being an adult with children of his own.

C) They all had a good laugh over the Devil's poor penmanship and the Devil confessed he'd been too hasty in wanting a child in the first place.

D) The shoemaker looked at the Devil, then at his child, then back at the Devil. He became quite concerned about the uncanny resemblance. He then looked at his wife, who averted her eyes.

Cynthia & the Chestnut Tree

The wicked stepmother did not care for her stepdaughter, Cynthia. She fussed over her two biological daughters from a previous marriage, but forced Cynthia to do all the difficult chores — brushing ash from the fireplace, dusting curtains, washing windows and melting lard into candles.

One day, the King announced there would be a great ball at the castle for all the single ladies. It was well known that his son, the Prince, was in search of a wife.

Cynthia's wicked stepmother prepared her two favorite daughters for the ball. They were adorned with jewellery and fitted with beautiful gowns. Cynthia asked if she, too, could attend the ball. Everyone laughed. "You can't go to the castle looking like *that*," they said.

When her stepmother and stepsisters rode away, Cynthia went outside and made a wish upon the magic chestnut tree. She wished…

A) That the carriage carrying her stepmother and stepsisters would drive off a cliff.

B) For there to be an easier, less smelly, way to make candles.

C) To be so beautiful that staring endlessly at her reflection in the mirror would be far more satisfying than attending some stupid ball.

D) Simply for her stepmother to love her, even just a
little.

The Weary Traveler

The weary traveler was making his way home from
war. It was winter. The land was covered with white
snow and blue ice. He followed a little-known short-
cut through the forest and spent the night inside a
cave, lying beside a warm fire, dreaming of beautiful
princesses, as weary travelers tend to do.

In the morning, he gathered his belongings to resume the journey home. Outside the cave, he stumbled
upon a rock buried in the snow. Beneath the rock was
a metal box. He lifted the box and undid the latch.
Inside he discovered…

A) A genie capable of granting three wishes to anyone who freed him. The genie, however, insisted
he was not trapped inside the box. He could have
gotten out at any time, no problem. He was simply resting.
B) A dead chipmunk, a chestnut, a pair of hair scissors and the brass key to a tower door.
C) A photograph of Cynthia lovingly embraced by
her stepmother.
D) All of the above and more.

Sirens

It came over all the city loudspeakers. *Prepare for the worst! Prepare yourselves. Ladies and gentlemen, prepare!* A small boy in short pants and polo shirt, walking beside his mother, clasped hands over his ears. The greasy, grey-whiskered drunk that regularly loiters outside TrueValue hardware gazed up, soberly contemplating the three tin speakers atop the tall metal pole. The farmer selling strawberries, sitting in his lawn chair along Hamilton Ave., kept right on reading *The Herald,* as if oblivious to the noise. Even my neighbor Lee did not pause his digging to heed the siren's monthly warning, though Lee believes he is the only one truly preparing for the worst by building a safety bunker. "When it happens, everyone will turn to me for help. And what am I suppose' to do? It's not like you weren't warned. That's what I'll say, before shutting my door on you all."

That was Lee's interpretation of the monthly alerts. Dig yourself a hole to hide in. My take was a bit different, not a call to prepare so much as a call to prepare to prepare. It was a preparation for the real preparation.

Not a *final* preparation. What good would a prepare system be if not properly prepared to prepare us. *Has anyone checked this thing?* someone might ask one day when it refuses to broadcast in an actual emergency. But by then it would all be too late. A prepare system not properly prepared is no good to anyone.

Each first Wednesday of the month at noon, I pause whatever activity I'm engaged in to acknowledge the broadcast's call for preparation and take note of my environment and those around me. Most people ignore the system. Some make snide complaints or furrow their brows in annoyance. I fear they are training themselves to dismiss the alert, tune it out altogether. When an actual emergency comes, they'll be sorry. We'll all be sorry.

I said as much to Lee. He shrugged. "There will always be those types," he said. "They can't be bothered. They refuse to think about it. They assume they'll naturally be ready when the time comes. That's human nature. You know the story about the ant and the grasshopper? They're dancing their time away. Not me. I'm getting ready. The final alarm is coming."

I knew Lee didn't like my idle, side-porch scrutiny of his efforts, but I enjoyed sitting and watching him criss-cross the yard with his red wheelbarrow, hauling dirt away to the empty lot beyond the fence line and back again. He will take particular joy in telling me during an actual catastrophe that I'm not allowed in that bunker of his. He will remind me how I sat with my pitcher of ice water and watched him haul dirt in the hot sun never once lifting a finger to help.

I'll say, "You're right, Lee. You're perfectly right. Now open that door, you fool. Let me in."

"Good day to you, Jay Cee."

Debbie is like clockwork. She comes every day at 12:15 with the mail. She hands it right to me if she sees I'm on the porch, which is where I usually am.

Debbie approached with her bright, lipstick-pink smile clutching a handful of assorted junk mail. She is never in such a rush she can't stop to exchange a few words. I often inquire about Turner, her son, an autistic. Most times she has something hopeful and inspiring to say. "He seems to have found himself a little girlfriend" or "I got a hug today" or "hippo-therapy has done wonders for him." On a bad day, she will wave off my question. "You know — always one crisis after another." I don't know how she deals with a boy like that on her own. And working as hard as she does.

"Everything fine at home?" I asked.

"Well, funny thing is I got an itch to pick up my old fiddle and Turner — he comes tearing into the bedroom when he hears me play. 'What's that, Mom!? What's that sound?' And he just sat there and watched me play like it was the most amazing thing." Debbie's eyes began to water. Her cheeks reddened and she quickly changed the subject.

"And you?" Debbie took the glass of water I handed her — "Ahhh. Thank you, Jay Cee" — and took a sip before continuing. "What's new around here? I see Lee's busy at work." Lee glanced up for a moment, as if he'd heard his name, but did not acknowledge us.

"You heard about the Mitchell girl, no?" I asked.

"Oh, Lord, yes. Yes. So sad."

"Makes you think, don't it?"

"True. Life is precious. Hold those dear close to you, Jay Cee. You never know when the time comes. Well, you have a great day. I gotta soldier on." She touched her fingers to the brim of her blue visors, like a salute, and climbed down the porch steps.

"The service is Sunday. See you there?"

She turned, gave a nod, saying, "Yup. I'll be there," then she continued walking back toward her mail cart.

This was the year of our city's centennial celebration. It was a matter of poor planning that during the award ceremony for the Junior Miss talent competition the city siren went off. The excitement surrounding the awards was deflated by the siren's cries to prepare. *Prepare yourself! Ladies and gentlemen, prepare!* People tried to talk over the warning. Some wandered away to get out of its deafening blare.

Bunny Mitchell, still in her bathing suit, stood shivering, waiting for the warnings to stop so she could receive her blue ribbon. Finally, the alert came to an end and Tony McAlastair returned to the microphone to re-commence the ceremony. He announced Bunny Mitchell's name to a smatter of applause. Bunny timidly stepped forward to take her place on the platform. Some say she appeared a bit ill and shaken, pale and scared.

I was there. I saw the whole thing. Her skinny legs stepped onto the platform. Her head and torso rose above the crowd. She looked frightened. Then she was gone, disappeared from view. Her fall should not have been serious. She didn't hit pavement, only turf. Yet she landed just so. And nothing could be done. Paramedics were on hand. They rushed to her side, checked her vitals, then placed her on a stretcher. She was gone by the time they reached St. Gemma's Hospital.

How do you prepare for something like that, I ask. Just a child. A freak accident.

I heard some talk. People saying, none of it would have happened if her parents had been there. Some blamed the MC for not walking her up the platform. Others decried the paramedic team, one of whom was a known drug abuser. But it seemed random to me. Just one of those things. A fall. Someone landed exactly the wrong way.

The ice clinked around in the glass pitcher as I poured. I placed the cup to my lips. My doctor said I need to drink more water. "You're drying up, old man." I'm afraid to drink too much water, though. Who knows what the hell they put in those reservoirs or whether the pipes are safe from contamination. I've heard stories. But I abide by the doctor's orders — though, warily.

Just then Lee started the engine on a giant cement mixer. Everything began to vibrate — my porch, my card table, my water glass — all resounding to the churn of machinery some fifty yards away.

I got off the porch and brought some water to Lee. Just to be neighborly. And to get an up-close look at the cement pouring.

"What's that?" Lee asked as I held out the glass.

"Water. Thought you might like some. It's hot out

today."

"What?"

I repeated myself louder this time to cut through the rumble of the mixer's gas motor.

He took the glass and drank.

"Where'd you buy that thing?" I asked, indicating the mixer.

"It's a rental."

"What's something like that cost to rent?"

"180 clams a day."

"Jesus, Lee. You're paying near 200 dollars a day on top of everything else?" I inspected the site. It had been weeks since I'd gotten a close look.

It was a good fifteen-foot drop. Steel rebar lined the sides. The muddy bottom was textured in boot prints and laid out with PVC piping. Two by fours marked off where each section of floor was to be poured.

Lee was taking this project more seriously than I first figured. Dumping all his money into a hole. "You're still driving that shit heap of a car, but you'll spend 200 dollars a day on a mixer? Lee, if you're so sure the world's going to hell, why not take what money you got and go travel? See the world while it's still there to see."

"Right. Fiddle away my time. No, sir. I'm in it to win it. I'm looking at the big picture. If you don't plan for the future you'll be stuck and buried in the past."

"Whose planning your boys' future? That's money I'm sure they could use for college."

Maybe I'm cruel to have mentioned his boys. I don't know why I did that. Can't keep my big mouth shut sometimes.

"Fuck you," said Lee. And walked away with my glass.

I didn't see Debbie at the Sunday service. But there were so many people. Half the town came to show support for the Mitchell family. The other half came to see what kind of parent drops their kid off at a talent competition and doesn't stick around to watch her win the damn thing. After the ceremony I lingered in the hall, hoping to run into Debbie.

Debbie didn't come around on Monday or Tuesday. There was no mail delivery at all. On Wednesday I caught sight of a young lady dropping letters into the mail slot on my front door. I hurried over from the side yard to get a word. She was a little thing with a horsey-brown ponytail and skinny, freckled arms. I asked what happened to Debbie. She didn't know. She was a new hire. She was still learning names. I said, "This is Debbie's route." She said it was hers now. She didn't know a Debbie.

"Who are you?"

She said her name was Kat. She'd recently graduated from Marsten Music College.

"And you're delivering mail?"

"Gotta start somewhere." She laughed. And I laughed, too, though not quite sure what was so funny about that.

"Nice to meet you, Mr. Aldrich. I better get back to my route." She threw the mail satchel over her shoulder and trotted away.

When Margaret passed, I thought my life was pretty much over. I felt an emptiness as wide as the sea. We'd been together for 39 years. We'd had our ups and downs, sure. But those years together changed me. Made us both better people. I didn't think it was possible to go on without her. My loneliness was so deep, I thought I was losing my mind, sometimes hearing a voice that weren't even there.

Then the worst thing imaginable happened: I went on. That emptiness got filled by other things. Tuesday poker with a group of fellow widowers. Cooking lessons at the PFV Hall. A new-found love of reading, particularly historical non-fiction. I found I wasn't thinking of Margaret every other moment, or even every other day. And that scared me. Is that all life is? A presence for so many years, then an absence. Then an absence filled by some entirely different presence.

After several weeks, I finally saw Debbie. She was with her son outside the IGA, pushing him in a wheelchair, both his legs in plaster bandages. She said he'd fallen out their apartment window. He was lucky to be alive. The post office had fired her for not coming to work. She found a lawyer, though, and was suing to get her job back.

"Somehow it will all work out," she said. Despite her obvious weariness, she maintained a smile. "But right now it's hard. I'm not going to lie. We have doctor bills, rent to pay — all that."

I went home and thought things over. I felt I could help in some way. I wanted to. I practically owed her. For several months after Margaret passed, those short daily conversations with Debbie were all I had to look forward to. It was the one thread still holding me to this world, to life, you know.

I slept on it. I had an idea. I took the scrap of paper with her number on it from my wallet and called. She couldn't say no. It made too perfect sense.

We were unloading Debbie and Turner's things from the rental truck when the alert system went off. *Prepare!* it shouted, as I lowered another box onto the pavement. "I don't want you lifting those," Debbie said, hurrying over to take the box and carry it to my front steps. *Ladies and Gentlemen, prepare yourselves.* The two of them did not own a whole lot. It took just one truck load. *Now is the time to be ready.* The only furniture was a futon mattress, a sofa and an old chester drawers. Everything else fit into several packing boxes and a bunch of plastic bags. *This has been a First Wednesday practice alert for the City of Lawndale. If this had been an actual emergency, this message would be followed by further instructions.*

Things were quiet next door. I hadn't seen much of Lee since I mentioned his sons, inflaming an old wound of his — divorce and custody battles — but the bunker appeared nearly complete. He'd re-sodded the lawn. Most of what was left concerned whatever wiring, organizing and decorating took place beneath the surface.

I'm not going to lie. That first couple months with Debbie and Turner in the house were rough. The kid tore strips of wallpaper off the living room walls while Debbie was out of the house and I was on the porch. He dumped pictures out of old photo albums. I found wedding photos of Margaret and me scattered on the carpet and under the sofa. He shat in the hallway one morning. Debbie tried to hide it, clean the mess, but I could still smell it. When I asked what happened, she was upfront and clear about how she intended to address the issue.

Things gradually became easier. It was a matter of time. Him getting used to my presence. A new home. Debbie got some part-time work at the IGA, while I kept an eye on Turner. He was off crutches by that time and getting around fine. Once he had his routine, things fell into an easy rhythm. He began to spend time on the porch with me, watching Lee's *goings on*, like a couple of old birders.

"There he is! That's his head peeking up. See it?"

"What's he doing?"

"He's laying some sort of wiring."

"For electricity?"

"Maybe. Or possibly an antenna of some sort."

"For a radio?"

"Could be. Maybe one of those Ham radios. You know what those are?"

One morning, I took my coffee to the porch and saw Turner talking to Lee over by the bunker. Lee was making all sorts of gestures with his arms, as if explaining his whole worldview. Indoctrinating the youngster in the Cult of Preparedness. Lee bent over and raised the lid off the bunker for Turner to peer down. *Come,* Lee gestured. And the two descended into the hole.

Kat came by with the mail. She'd begun to relax and take her route more slowly. She didn't mind stopping to chat a bit. She thought I was doing a great thing taking Debbie and Turner into my house.

"Ain't like that," I told her. "A guy my age shouldn't live alone. It's practical all around."

"Still..." she said, squinting her eyes and giving me a devilish smile. We both did one of those laughs again where she's thinking something funny and I'm just confused, but laughing along anyway.

No one thought the First Wednesday warning system would ever come to an end. Mostly, because no one ever thought to end it. It seemed something we needed to bear with, something doing us a decency, even if hardly no one paid it any mind. It was Kat who took the petition around.

"What's all this about?"

"Like I said — the monthly siren. You may have noticed it."

"I'm old. I'm not deaf."

"We're collecting signatures to end it. It's an antiquated system. And a major annoyance."

"Sometimes we need to put up with a little annoyance for the greater good."

"Ya. If there was a greater good involved. But, like I said, it's an antiquated system. There are more effective ways to spread warnings. We're all connected to the internet. And there's radio and TV still. That thing was put up long before everyone carried a phone in their pocket."

"You're screwing with a venerable, long-standing city tradition."

"You're messing with me, aren't you, Mr. Aldrich?"

I took her clipboard and signed. Of course I was

all too willing to get rid of the damn thing. "Whose idea was this?"

Kat took the clipboard from me. "Mine," she said. "See you tomorrow, Mr. A." She shoved the clipboard into her satchel and headed toward the next house.

"Tomorrow's Saturday," I hollered after her.

She turned her head, replying over her shoulder. "The city fair," she shouted. "You promised you'd come hear my group perform."

I didn't make it to the city fair. Turner was there, though. Lee took him. They had front-row seats next to empty chairs, places reserved for me and Debbie. I was at St. Gemma's. Debbie was at my bedside. I'd had a stroke in the middle of the night. Debbie was concerned when I hadn't gotten up for breakfast. She checked in on me, knew immediately something was wrong, and called 911.

I couldn't speak. I couldn't move more than fingers and eyelids. In surgery, they had stuck something way deep inside me to remove the clotting, then wheeled me into intensive care to keep me under observation. Debbie stayed beside my bed. She held my fingers, but moved away whenever the nurses were busy trying to get at me with their needles, tubes and wires.

"Everything is going to be okay, Jay Cee," Debbie said. Always hopeful, that girl. I knew it wasn't true, though. Air whispered in and out my throat. Something beneath my abdomen began to spasm, trying to shake itself free. I felt my body loosening, a sense of letting go. It was okay. It wasn't entirely a bad feeling.

I started to apprehend strange noises. *Do you hear that?*

"What is it, Jay Cee? You want to tell me something?"

The music. Do you hear music? My god. Listen to that, would you?

"You're going to be fine. Jay Cee? Jay Cee? Nurse!"

I thought I was vocally responding, but the words were only in my head. Not the music, though. It was out there, coming closer. As it grew louder, the room turned dark. Everything went black. In that complete darkness, I kept listening until, finally, I saw a spot of light. The light opened like an aperture. The city fairground appeared below me, its amusement rides and carnival games and people carrying fried meats on plates and skewers, and confectionery sweets in cups and cones.

Directly beneath me was the festival stage, with its wood platform, metal scaffolding, amplifiers and hanging lights. A crowd of people occupied a dozen rows of folding chairs before the stage. Many more sat on colorful blankets atop the berm.

I immediately spotted Turner and Lee up front, with two empty chairs beside them, the ones meant for Debbie and me. Behind them were pals of mine from Tuesday poker nights. Surrounding them were others I recognized. People from my PFV Hall cooking class. Pastor Lynd, seated next to the Mitchells, Bradley and Sue. Francis Jacoby, my former boss at Honeywell, seated between his long-time partner, Avery, and Margaret's cousin Flo. Next to Flo was her husband Jeffrey, mopping his bald head with a hanky. I was surprised how many of them were people I knew. Guess that's part of living in a small city.

The performers on stage were school kids, retirees, dads and moms, college undergrads home for the summer, various workers from around town — waitresses, cooks, the guy who parks cars at the White Hall Building, the lady at the Save-On who always gave me a "preferred customer" discount, two of the tellers from Wells Fargo, Billy, the owner of Captain Jack's ice-cream shack...A motley bunch of amateur musicians and singers.

Leading them all was Kat, waving her conductor's baton, keeping them in time with the score. It was a lengthy composition she had dismissively referred to as "some little ditty," when extending me an invitation to the performance.

I can't describe the music. It was both familiar and continually unexpected in the way its melody kept repeating and changing. Sounded like something I'd heard all my life, but hadn't a clue from when or where exactly.

Kat struggled with the baton, dropping it twice. She was not much of a conductor. The musicians, apparently, had practiced enough to hold it together despite her faulty baton work. Clearly, Kat was a bit out of sorts. Nerves, I suppose. Her face was puffy, red. Eyes swollen as if heavy with tears.

Oddly, there were many teary-eyed folks in the crowd. True music lovers. Overcome with emotion. Even Lee, sitting stiff and upright, quickly wiped away an occasional tear. Sue Mitchell was sobbing into her husband's lapel. Avery kept handing cousin Flo tissues to dry her eyes. I had no idea how deeply these people loved music. It was amazing to behold. Their heads nodded. Hands reached for one another. Bodies swayed. Horns pulsed. Strings resounded. Vibrations entered and sympathised within each and all, as if every heart were playing its very own part.

If such harmony as this was the last Earthly sound I ever heard, I believe I could happily die in peace.

Ye Olde Swan

To-morrow! There will be drinking and dancing at Ye Olde Swan. Carriage cars of the land's finest folk shall flock there to fest and digest and take part in the annual Dance Contest. It's a tradition spanning some three centuries. Count 'em. Three. Always the talk. Setting trends for ages to come. The gowns and laces. The blackened boots. Hairs coiffed, crimped and creamed. The bilious beards bourne proudly — each year, rich innovations in whisker technology, titillation and tantalization! Anyone who's anyone shall gather for a gander at Ye Olde Swan.

Bridget Yule will be there. Mark my word. Not something she'd miss for a million Ducats or a half-eaten fig. Her fine, muscular calves will deign to attend, cemented firmly beneath her cleaved, bottom end. Look at her bend! Of course Yule sadly lost last season's competition to Sonya F. Sonya Figgis now Sonya Stiggs. Malcolm Stiggs staked three months wages for the win, thus receiving her hand in matrimony along with the seven-to-one odds prize winning purse. Was there a cheat? Did blacken monies pass hand between judges, contenders and bettors? Well, why not ask were there clandestine members of the Ancient Noble Order of the Gormogons dressed in drag? Were rats, bedecked in firework-laden capes released beneath the floorboards and air grates? Were ales spiked with Limesworth Callings and other psychotropic elixirs? Did Bagman Haupmunster reveal the mystery of Shangsworth Hall held secret for so many centuries, causing Lyra Trippleton to faint flat upon the garlands? These are only reported rumours. Mere speculation. Those who fled in the uproar of dust clouds, shattered glass, squeals, urine, vomit and lunging apparitions were not entirely sure what had been seen or not seen, said or unsaid.

All I can add, as dutiful documentarian of deeds, is last year's festivities left a high-water mark upon Ye Olde Swan's weathered shingles — a culmination of events from which no one has yet fully recovered, particularly not Acron Foulmouth, former and possibly current Proprietor and Chief of Ye Olde Swan Properties & Holdings. There are those who swear Falmouth perished, suffocated within the massive clouds of vapour that swept over the property immediately after the frenzied herd of shaved and painted swine smashed through the lattice gates, tore up the groundwork and chased menstruating young misses into the brackish waters of the Lacerta Canal. Who had painted the swine in runic symbols, bold stripes and the Eye of Providence? What toxicity composed those nimbus clouds of gas? Did Acron Foulmouth indeed perish? Then who was that man at Prigg's Crossing the following autumn dressed in a grey tunic and herringbone pleats, who many swore oath was indeed Foulmouth, his very self — yet the man refused to answer by name and continued to bark, growl and whimper as if possessed by some sorrowful hound?

These are only some of the many mysteries surrounding that evening's dance competition. And this year's event promises to inspire even more philandry, festoonery and diabolism. Who would miss such an affair? Not Camille Henrot-Clegg. Surely not. For she has already commissioned a fine gossamer gown for the evening's competition. I have personally seen plans which call for trained doves to hold aloft ribbons and veil, and sketches detailing a *pouf l'amour wig*, concealing a miniature propane tank emitting fierce blue flames. But will that suffice for the win? Can it possibly compete with the inimitable Gracy Frenchman and her imaginative cunning and uncanny flare for fashion? Her designs are said to be so secretive, even her own seamstress is made to work blindfold. Unsubstantiated rumour suggests her attire for this year's competition involves a saltwater tank and a frenzy of live baby sharks.

INSERT ADVERTISEMENT HERE FOR FINE LOCAL FISHMONGER & PHLEMATORIUM

I ask once more, Who would miss such an opportunity to attend? Nay, who could scarcely dare not to attend, compulsory as it is for all virgins, chevaliers and Accolades of the Seventh Neon Throne. The stakes are high. Higher than Moe Grecian's hairline circa 1854. Higher still than the dangling gold tassels of Ye Olde Swan's razor sharp ceiling fans. Losers shall be force- fed leftovers until their inseams part way. And winners be forever immortalised as bronze figurines enclosed within the glass display case in the Ye Olde Swan reception alcove.

INSERT PHOTO (SEE THIS YEAR'S EVENT BROCHURE TO SELECT POSSIBLE INTERIOR PHOTOGRAPHS)

For sure, Scotty Nickerson (Ol' Scotty Nix, by which he is most commonly mentioned) will be on hand, despite his murder some one hundred and thirty-seven years gone. Ol' Scotty Nix, cursed as he is to return year after year, never fails to attend the annual Dance Contest, often partnering with Lola Foulmouth, the great Acron matriarch, who ceased to wither and age decades long past, thus ensuing the eternal blossoming of her fourteenth year. There is no pair I've seen or not seen who can quite clear a dance floor like those two. All agree, no sight moistens the sentimental eye like that of an ancient shadow of a man sweeping the dance floor with his un-aging child bride apparition.

As per tradition, all past winners will dutifully attend, either bodily or by reflective mirror. The judges? As hooded, faceless beings, it is certainly difficult to detect any change in council from year to year. But, rest assured, they remain as constant as the bright Cygnus stars in the night sky above and the ever-melting iron core beneath Earth's mantle.

Without Judges, the Dance Contest would revert to mere popular opinion, as in days of yore. Such popular vote, not balanced by judicial prudence, as all agree, would be sheer Anarchy. [History buffs amongst us may recall the 1837 Dance Contest in which popular vote vastly differed from that of our judges. Yes, it is true! It did happen! Which is why precautions are now taken so any popular vote be repeated until results harmoniously align with those of our Judges. In fact, this is the very reason why we now refer to popular ballots as *returns*!]

INSERT PROMOTIONAL GRAPHIC FOR NEXT MONTH'S FEATURE: TOP 10 NATURAL DISASTERS YOU CAN RECREATE AT HOME.

Let us dispel all rumour that this years Dance Contest will be the last of its sort. Preposterous, to say the least. Speculation that Ye Olde Swan does not exist and never did exist is simply that — speculation. Speculation, commentary, hearsay and chattery. It is simply impossible to hold the thought of its non-existence in one's mind, particularly when we have each heard and read so much of its goings-on and felt its elemental forces deep within our own flesh and bone.

If centuries of slavish coverage devoted to the Dance Contest and its attendees be not proof enough of its existence for some, what more can I offer? Have we not, each and everyone, been accosted on the road by some lost soul in search of the Swan? Have we not all heard the music, glimpsed the fairy lights? Harkened the thunderous hoof beats marking time? Observed the sway of inebriated tall grass, the circling conspiracy of ravens, a blackening cloud of wings? Have we all not surveyed, with naked eye, the aurora's tally of lights, signifying each judicious score, nor witnessed the spectral blaze proclaiming each year's winning pair? Have we not each felt a fervent chill crawl through flesh as the departing guests rush home, fleeing from the approaching dawn, which threatens to tear them limb from limb as it ushers in the next tomorrow? How then can there be any doubt Ye Olde Swan will once more reprise its gore as it lifts its wings and opens its doors?

The Silver Leaf

Dear Mr. Hobart.

I would be the happiest person on Earth if you would allow me to return to The Silver Leaf. I do not necessarily expect to resume my former position as desk clerk nor receive anything near my previous wages. I realize I will need to regain your trust and prove my worthiness once more. But if you allow me a fresh start, I will happily take any position offered, day or night shift, full or part time. Bussing tables in the dining hall would suit me fine. Even linen service. Or temporary maintenance work. I know you have been considering re-carpeting the badly stained second and third floor landings. I have experience removing old carpeting and would gladly do this for far less than a professional carpet service. I could also undertake window cleaning or any ground work that needs doing — weeding, raking, pruning, excavating — what have you.

I understand I will need to work hard to calm any anxieties my former colleagues may have in regard to working with me again. But I am confident once I return to duty they will appreciate the extra steps I'm willing to take to make everyone's job easier. I have learned a lot from past mistakes and I am certain similar mishaps will not repeat themselves. As for those who stood against me, I hold no grudge nor harbor any resentment. I have them to thank, actually, for helping to turn my life around. Especially Angela Murphy.

Angela, I understand, has stated publicly there is "no way in Hell" you and the owners of The Silver Leaf would allow me back. But I have always had a good working relationship with you in the past. And I believe the owners are open-minded individuals. I regret not having fully disclosed previous employment difficulties on my job application, but at the time I believed it would unjustly prejudice any hiring decisions. I know now that was wrong of me. Over my many months of service, I came to see The Silver Leaf as a more tolerant and thoughtful employer than I had first given credit.

My doctors and The State of Delaware have all concluded I am perfectly fit to resume my former life and endeavours as long as I continue to receive treatment for my condition. As it was clearly presented in court, my behavior was entirely hormonal and had nothing whatsoever to do with the night sky. Because of all the mayhem, fuss and confusion, Angela and the others most certainly misapprehended what occurred. Maybe a trick of moonlight had given the appearance I had somehow changed form. Maybe it was all shadow and befuddlement. As my attorney clearly demonstrated in court, fear can often affect judgement and perception. I'm sure you, Mr. Hobart, like most rational people, are not superstitious in nature. Certainly you would never place credulity in stories of the supernatural such as werewolves!

Believe me, there is no one who holds The Silver Leaf in as high a regard as I. With its long history of excellent service, ground security and complete discretion, The Silver Leaf has maintained a sterling reputation over the years. Few other inns can hold a torch to its standing. I am fortunate to have been part of such an honourable legacy. And, though Angela may not believe it, I have always considered it, indeed, a high privilege to work there. And for you.

I would be most grateful for an opportunity to speak further about this matter in person and answer any questions you may have in regard to the series of incidents leading to the blood-stained carpeting and my subsequent mandatory confinement. I shall return to your area on the near solstice. Please inform me of your availability. I would be pleased to meet at your convenience, either at The Silver Leaf or a proximate location of your preference.

I hope this letter finds you well and in full recovery.

Yours truly,

Linda Kramer

Canada

She had a perfect, undamaged face, as if she kept her face sealed in a contamination free, moisturized pouch when not in use. In office meetings, she always came prepared. Numerous charts, graphs, tables, diagrams, handouts. We tried to listen. *Really*. But, instead, focused on the mouth, the moist lips, the quick tongue flicks, the drooping vowels, the clack of consonants. When she stopped speaking, we'd just stare. Not quite sure what had been said. Or not said.

Stacy Shaw, division manager, often broke the long, awkward silence with a "Thank you, Ellen," before asking for comments. We'd gaze down at hands and feet. Shuffle papers. Shrug *whatevers*. Anything to keep our eyes off that face.

Ellen was not here during the crisis. She came afterwards. I'm guessing from North Canada. But no one can say for sure. Human Resources normally keeps track of such things, but I asked Barbara Fisher about Ellen and learned no one had bothered to check references or personal history. Ellen interviewed with several key managers, but all anyone could recall was the face, the wispy brows, the pink eyelids, the jawline, the orbed chin. Chin like a boiled egg. A sexy boiled egg. Or how I remembered boiled eggs used to be.

Her cubby was along the hall and to the left, near the back of the building. It had a scenic view — the rolling hills, covered in dead wildflowers and old refrigerators. Some of us ate lunch out there. We sat on the dead refrigerators, unwrapped sandwiches from the Jimmy Mart, sipped bottled energy milk or containers of machine coffee. We ate mostly in silence. If we spoke, it was to complain about the weather, the smells or the voices in our heads. We'd glance up at the third floor. Does she watch us? If the window glass wasn't opaque, we would watch her. I would anyway. I suspect others wanted to keep an eye on her too. We're all thinking the same thing. Why her and not us? How does she get away with a face like that?

It was the crisis that did this. Wrecked the best thing we had going. Our faces. We got through it, though. Some of us. *La dee dee. La dee da. Life goes on.* If it wasn't for wrecked faces, our skin irritations, scales and growths, you'd never know we suffered. Yes, we suffered. Hell, we suffered. Doctors, nurses and beauticians said don't dwell on it. Don't pick at it. There is plenty more living to do. Just keep away from mirrors.

Ellen rose quickly in rank. By mid-February she was elected head of the Maelstrom project. She joked about the name. *Maelstrom.* "I'm supposed to manage a Maelstrom? Good luck to me!" She laughed inappropriately. Often. Not that there was ever an appropriate moment to laugh. Her smiles destroyed us. Her giggles made us want to hurt something. Ourselves mainly.

When Ellen began overseeing our work, she became difficult to avoid. Most managers would memo their requests or scribble them on a smudge board with a grease stick. But Ellen was big on facetime. Maybe that was a Canadian thing. Or maybe she was sadistic. In response, people began to cream up. Tubs of facial jelly kept in desk drawers. Caked-on makeup. Waxed lips. Penned eyebrows. Pitiful attempts to cover scars, sores, lumps, rashes and discoloration. But each fix only drew more attention to the problem.

Ellen had a lot of questions. For me, they were about the 3-Sector panels I commissioned. And about the trial numbers I generated. And about the variations in cross-sector habitats that had been formulated during the quadrennial economic sequestration. Sometimes she was at my cubby three or four times a day. I could not get used to it. The sound of her voice startled me each time. A glance at her face made my pits dampen, hands tremble, face swell, and heart gurgle like a draining estuary.

"What's up, Ace?" Ellen said. Third time that day. Not even noon. "Sorry," she said. "I need to start knocking."

I took a moment to gather my cool. *Don't look up*, I told myself. *Focus on her hands. Her collar. Her vestment. Her wedged pantoons.* It did not work, though. My eyes immediately went to the face. They locked on. They froze. I could not unfasten them. That face. That damn face. It seemed weird it was always the same.

Never crumbled, fell apart, swam adrift, shifted askew or slackened. Just solid, smooth, complete. Like something from an old Hollywood film or Renaissance portrait. The sort of face that once inspired songs, poetry, dance and adultery.

"Awesome shirt," she said. "That's a great pattern. Kind of retro."

I tried saying thanks, but slather caught in my throat pipe. I coughed out something grey-blue. Ellen evaded the projectile phlegm and went on speaking.

"Look here," she said, hefting a stack of paper. "I found last year's associate members catalog behind the radiation flow jets. Some of these could go onto the new reintegration list." She heaved the stack into my hands, adding, "Oh. And can you give me the numbers you assigned for those reflector panels?"

"3-Sector panels?"

"Right. That's what I meant."

"Sure. I'll send a doc this afternoon."

"Any chance getting that before lunch-ola?"

"Will do. No problem."

"Thanks, doll!"

Off she went. *Doll?* Was she trying to sound retro or just mocking me? Was that an expression Canadians still used? If anyone was doll-faced around here it was her. The rest of us looked like something chewed over, dragged through dirt and sludge and left in the sun to curdle.

Doesn't seem fair people like Ellen still exist. Pretty much everyone who hadn't lost their looks in the crisis had left. Or were taken. They began disappearing amidst the upheaval. We assumed many were kidnapped, sold, shipped overseas. Then some started appearing on our screens. They would be dressed in bright tunics and suede vestments, hair pulled back in bungels, reading updates on the crisis. Or they'd be cheerfully selling masks, ammunition, hydraulic water pumps, prophylactic liniments and salves. Sometimes they were acting in instructional videos, like DIY bone repair, auto assembly and organ harvesting. Often they were spotted as audience members or contestants in talent competitions and game shows.

We never heard back from those who left. No replies to our numerous calls, missives and inquiries. We felt abandoned. Our faces got worse. The voices in our heads grew louder. After a time, the broadcast feeds became disrupted. Perhaps from solar flares or other natural forces. Some thought it was intentional; Topeka was abandoning us. Eventually, all we had was bad audio. Audience laughter. Jazz fusion guitar. Interviews with emissaries. Stories of victorious dark horses. Noise. Static. Applause. Dead air.

Every day there would be another series of questions or requests from Ellen. And each time she would have something to say about my appearance. Remarks about my hair. My shirts. My ankle guards. My leggings.

"I've been waiting for argyle to make a comeback," she said. "Sorry, that probably sounded mean. I meant I love argyle, but nobody wears it any more. You notice that? It's cool that you have argyle leggings. That's all I'm saying."

Even when flustered, her face possessed a confidence no words could match. She showed me portrait photos of the engineers and designers working on Maelstrom. The photos were for a catalog. She wanted the Emissaries to realize they're purchasing components *made by real people, for real people.* That was her big marketing idea. *Made by real people, for real people.* Somehow the slogan was approved. Or maybe it wasn't. Maybe she put it up for approval and everyone simply glanced at her face and nodded.

The photos were good. Professionally taken. Warm lighting. Soft focus. A narrow depth of field. An impressionistic background that could have been either tawny burlap or midday sky. If it wasn't for the hideous faces, you'd think they were licensed spokesmodels or Emissaries.

"Great." I handed them back.

"Thanks, Ace!"

One day, while leaving the building, Jody said, "You and that Ellen got something going?" First, I thought he was referring to the Maelstrom project. Then it occurred he meant something else. I wasn't sure if he was serious or *har har*-ing me.

Jody was my closest friend at work. Maybe "friend" is overstating it. We didn't hang out after hours. But we often sat on the same refrigerator at lunch. Sometimes we spoke for a minute or two in the parking lot before heading home. I knew Jody was married. Had two kids. Showed me photos. Ugly, but no uglier than other people's kids. Certainly better-looking than the feral scavenger ones. Weird that Jody even kept photos. Or showed them to anyone. What were we expected to say? *Well, Jody, aren't they something!*

"She's at your desk a lot, talk an' laughin', like y'all's up to some monkey business? I'm only jus' askin'."

"That's not laughing, Jody. That's chortling. That's her mocking me to my face. It would be pretty weird if there was anything going on between us other than work."

"Well, it ain't just me who's wonderin'." He nodded toward the clouds. Then waved goodbye and boarded his shambles. As he drove off, a voice in my head spoke. *Individual responsibility is the flower of social decency.*

I had converted a large closet in my apartment into a safe room. The walls and ceiling were covered with magnetic strips. It was the evening of the Blood Moon. At 11:30 pm, I went into my safe space and lit a cranberry-scented candle. I sang the Blood Moon song.

> *Not me*
> *Not me*
> *Oh red moon*
> *Oh howling moon*
> *Take the children*
> *Take trees*
> *Take the sun*
> *Just don't take me*
> *No, not me*

Around midnight, there grew a distant rumbling. Floorboards trembled. A couple strips of magnet fell from the ceiling. I pressed them back in place. A loud, painful sigh, like twisting metal, grew louder. Heat radiated from the magnets. Sweat ran from beneath my hair follicles into the raw patches surrounding my eyeholes and into my eyes. My arms ached from holding the magnets in place, but I feared letting go. *Hold on*, I told myself. *Just a few minutes more.*

Then it passed. I knelt and gave thanks. I imagined hundreds of others doing the same — heads bowed humbly, grateful to be spared once more. At 1 a.m., I rubbed cold cream over my face and hands, threw on a white tunic and left the building.

Outside everything was quiet except for the clatter of opening and closing doors, gates and hole covers. The sidewalks filled with people dressed in white. Yellow stars and a red moon illuminated every tunic, robe, vestment and gown. We raised our moisturized faces to the sky and breathed deep, letting the cold air fill our chest cavities. No one spoke a word.

For twenty minutes, we just stood there, breathing in the cool air, until the sirens roared. Then we returned to our homes. Some to sleep. Some to feast. I treated myself to microwave pojay bacon crisps and drank a jar of fermented rice husk. Around 5 a.m. the burnt sky began to renew itself. I shook bits of blackened crisps from my tunic, undressed and lay in bed. I fell asleep to the lull of voices gently whispering to me, *Quality is job number one.*

Friday, when we returned to work, everything seemed fine. Nearly normal. No talk about the moon. Not that we ever talked about such things. But on this morning, everyone was particularly quiet. Ellen, usually one of the first to arrive, was missing. Had someone not told her about the Blood Moon? Had no one warned her to stay indoors?

There was a 10:30 meeting scheduled for middle management. Ellen had wanted me to attend with her. I watched Jay Bartos gather papers and fixatives, getting ready to head to the conference room downstairs. Laura Singer picked up her slate and neck purse and pursued Jay to the stairwell. The clock displayed 10:24 in glowing orange numbers. No Ellen. 10:25. Had I misunderstood? Was I supposed to meet her downstairs? 10:26. Scuffles came from the stairwell. Ellen appeared in the hall, walking fast in rubber cow shoes. She threw her belly bag on her desk and bee-lined toward me.

"Oh man. I'm late today. You ready, Ace? Let's do this."

On the smudge board in the conference room Ellen wrote PRAXIS and ADAPTATION. There were many arrows, numbers and boxes. Her lips moved quickly. Her eyes darted back and forth between the board and the group of nine managers seated at the conference table. We tried to avoid looking directly at her. I imagine we were all thinking the same thing. *What did she do Wednesday night? Why is she happy? Does she even know how beautiful her face is?*

I stayed later than usual Friday. I wanted to finish calculating the repayment costs on the 3-Sector panel implementation studies. That's what I told myself, anyway. Really, I just wanted to keep an eye on Ellen. She was often one of the last to leave. I assumed she drove the shambles made from Camry and Civic parts with a wrought iron grill welded atop its roof. But Jody claimed he once saw her get out of a Tri-Tower pickup taxi and maybe didn't drive at all.

Ellen had her jackover on, belly pack over one shoulder, ready to leave for the day, when she peeked into my cubby. "Working late, Ace?"

"Ya. Finishing this up," I said, sliding some papers around on my desktop.

"Great. Got big plans for the weekend?"

I hesitated before speaking, unsure if Ellen even knew about The Lake. "Well, I'll be going to The Lake tomorrow."

"Oh, *The Lake*," she said. "I heard about that. What is it you do there?"

"It's just a thing. We're supposed to go Saturdays, get in the water, dry off in the sun." I shrugged as if it were no big deal. Nothing at all, really.

Ellen's eyes searched my face before resting their gaze somewhere around my neck and chest. The right corner of her lips quivered slightly. The black of her pupils expanded, nearly enveloping the blue of her irises. *Stop it!* I told myself. *You're staring.* I turned away, looked at my hands, pressed my finger tips together. Ellen bent down, held her face to mine. She was smiling again. "That sounds like fun," she said. "Would you mind if I came?"

On the drive home I was in a panic. For some reason I agreed to pick Ellen up Saturday morning. Drive her to The Lake. What was I thinking? People would notice. Notice me with her. They'd think, *What is she doing? Who does she think she's kidding? She needs our lake like the moon needs more radon stations.*

Don't act worried, I reminded myself. If they see you worried, they'll send someone to visit you at work.

Ask you to complete a questionnaire. Everyone says, *No big deal. The Emissaries are looking out for you.* But I know someone who apparently failed her questionnaire and went missing for several years. By chance, I saw her selling bottled lake water behind the old Expo Center. She was dirty, tattered and yellow, liked she'd been spending too much time in the Free Enterprise Zone. She sat in the shade with tiny glass vials laid out on a blanket. Failure to report someone selling lake water was a crime. I avoided her eyes. Hurried past. Someone else would invariably report her — if Skeye security cameras hadn't already caught eye of her behavior.

When I drove my shambles to Ellen's building, she was waiting outside, dressed in a long tan skire and donning a light blue Nylette jackover with white clasps. Two Savvy Jones shopping bags hung at her sides. She set one down, opened the door and got in.

"This is nice," she said, examining the interior of my shambles. "Did you build it yourself?"

"Yup. It's sort of a hybrid GrandAm, Caterpillar, Rover. The hood is from an old carnival fun ride.

"I love it!" Ellen smiled and buckled herself into the car seat.

We drove past the bluffs overlooking Randy Valley and the unregistered zones, then up the Piscador hillside, past the sulphur pits, the KLS crash site, the lime-green runoff from Bradley Mines, and the sludge pond that, despite its electrical fencing and razor wire, couldn't keep feral children from climbing inside and devouring the nematodes and milk thistle.

"I've never been up this way," Ellen said. She seemed excited, as if everything here was oddly beautiful to her.

"I'm sure Canada is much nicer than this."

"Canada? You think I'm from Canada?" She giggled. "Why would you think that?"

I didn't want to bring up her face. I probably should have dropped the subject. Instead I said something like how she didn't look like the rest of us.

"How do you mean? How do I look?"

My tongue began to swell. My cheeks burned prickly beneath their scars. Sores almost healed ached to part open. I made some weird noises, then coughed to cover their sound, coughed like something had gone down the wrong throat pipe.

"You okay?"

I nodded, trying to breathe steady.

"I hope this doesn't sound vain," Ellen said, a hand holding tight to the dash as we rumbled over shattered deflector panels and charred drone bodies. "But I'm curious how others see me. I don't know what I look like. I have what's called *prosopagnosia*. It's a brain disorder. I can't recognise faces. Not even my own. Weird, huh?"

"Proso...pah — boy, that's a mouthful."

"It's greek for *unknowable face*. Maybe you've noticed. It's why I sometimes confuse people's names."

I hadn't noticed.

"I don't have a problem recognizing you, though," she said. "You always dress sharp and you have a nice smell." She turned toward me. I held stiff, eyeholes fixed on the road. The pavement was growing dangerous with its widening cracks. Gaping fissures along the road shoulder could consume an entire wheel of a Helm Crusher.

We drove uphill until reaching the park gates. The wood sign fixed to the stone pillars was weathered and splintered. It had previously read CAVERNUS METROPARK, but now appeared more like AVERNUS NEΓRO ARK.

I slowed the shambles to almost a complete stop. It suddenly occurred to me how wildly inappropriate this was.

"Everything okay?" Ellen asked.

"Maybe this wasn't such a good idea. Are you sure you want to go?"

"I'd love to visit The Lake. But if you don't want — "

"It's only..." I hesitated before continuing. "It's sort of a ritual and stuff. You might think it weird. People take off clothes, get in the water. Not something you have to do, though. Just...I probably should have mentioned all this before."

Ellen smiled reassuringly. "It's okay. I know it's one of your customs, the way people do things here. I'm curious. I'd like to see."

Several shambles and long-haul trail treaders were coming up from behind. I accelerated through the gates and into the park. We rode amidst the ribs of dead oak spines and rust-needle evergreens. Vehicles, both behind and ahead, raised clouds of yellow dirt. We covered our faces with neck collars and sleeves to prevent dust from filling our nostrils and throats.

We followed the other vehicles toward Cavernus Lake. At the lake's perimeter, the shambles and treaders ahead of us turned right, while I swung left, heading toward the lake's less-visited shoreline and parking area.

I drove the shambles behind several rusted oil barrels and parked it beside a mountainous stack of mouldering pressboard furniture and some nastily stained foam mattresses. Ellen took her things out of the back seat.

"I brought lunch," she said, indicating one of the Savvy Jones shopping bags. "I made some fried pasta salad. And there's some pojay sandwiches. I hope you like pojay."

The old Wesley Pojay jingle sounded off in my head. *No one makes pojay, like Wesley makes pojay, 'cuz only Wesley's Pojay is the best.*

"It's the best," I said. "Thank you."

I removed a fleece blanket and a rifle from the trunk of my shambles. I slung the rifle over one shoulder and carried the blanket around my neck. "This way," I said, leading Ellen past the old mattresses and along a narrow path through pine needles, snake webs, shino scat and thorny bramble.

The Lake was calm. Its milky ochre surface reflected the clouds above like the patina on an old mirror. Black froth framed its edges. In the distance, far beyond the spindles of dead forest, you could make out the nine towers in the haze. Tall enough to nearly reach the clouds. It's amazing they still stand, though possibly no one has inhabited them in years.

I kicked away a few cans, tangled wires and dry branches to clear a space for us. We weren't the only ones who had chosen the reclusive side of The Lake, but everyone here kept a respectful distance. Most were already undressed. Or partially undressed. They laid on their backs gazing up at the sky. Or they sat, knees out front, eyes fixed upon the sallow-hued lake.

Ellen didn't bring a blanket. Another thing I had forgotten to mention. I offered to share mine. I spread it out, then searched for a good place to lay my rifle. Stalling really. I got nervous about undressing in front of her.

Ellen, aware of the naked people in the near distance, didn't hesitate to undress. Her feathery, white hair flung asunder as she pulled her head through the neck of her jackover. Her skire and underprops dropped to her ankles. She kicked them onto the blanket.

I stepped away and rested my rifle against a piece of old, rusted irrigation pipe, trigger up. A voice in my head repeated the phrase *Capital gains are God's gift*, over and over.

Ellen began speaking, but I quickly touched her arm and pressed a finger to my lips. "Please don't speak," I whispered. I turned to see if anyone was watching. There was an old man. Thin and stoop-shouldered. Reddish purple and black tattoos covered nearly his entire body, except the face. He turned his head and scowled at us. I lowered my eyes. *Capital gains are God's gift*, continued the voice inside my brain.

The Lake changed plenty since I was a kid. There used to be picnic tables and grills, sand and grass. Grey squirrels and ruby chipmunks ran along branches and scurried beneath bramble. Last time Dad and I came, he'd brought Claire with him. And a bucket of fried chicken parts. Real parts. Claire spread out a blanket, while Dad unloaded the cooler from the back of his truckette.

We knelt and prayed before eating. Dad spoke. "We thank Thee for your bounty and for this meal with which we are about to consume and the freedom from which it is made." *Amen*, we replied and tore into the chicken parts.

After lunch, Dad took off his t-shirt and shorts, revealing a swimsuit underneath. "I'm going to work off that chicken," he said, slapping his big white belly.

"You can't swim. You just ate," said Claire.

Dad made a puffing noise with his mouth and gave a "never you mind" wave of his hand. To me he said, "Let's see if old Dad can make it to the other side and back." He cracked his knuckles and frog-marched toward the water.

I was going to follow him, but Claire stopped me. "You need to wait thirty-minutes." I was too young to not listen to her, even though she wasn't my mom and had no right telling me what to do.

Claire carried the plastic containers and paper plates toward the rubbish bins. The bins were overflowing, so she set everything on the ground amidst a pile of styrofoam take-out containers and Skeye High beer cans. She returned to the blanket and took a paperback book out of her BP Pharma tote bag.

"I'm going to read for a bit." She pulled out a feather bookmark. "I'm getting to my favorite section."

I took off my t-shirt and laid back. I watched the clouds pull apart and recombine form. When I tired of that, I rolled onto my stomach and watched an ant slowly crawling through the dirt. Nature is kind of boring, I thought. I wanted to bring a game player, but Dad wouldn't let me. "A little break from technology is what we need," he said. *We* meaning *he*.

I turned my head sideways to peer at Claire from beneath my arm bottom. She was wearing a bikini top that barely hid her enormous nipples. I don't know where Dad met Claire. I found her in the kitchen one morning eating Gorilo wafers and drinking a can of I Dream of Coffee. She shook my hand. "Hello, Eddie. I'm Claire. I'm a friend of your father's."

Claire lowered her book. "Are you staring at my boobs?"

I shut my eyes. "No," I said.

"They're not real, you know."

I lowered my arm and looked. Claire peered down into her own cleavage. "I had a boob job when I was eighteen." She squeezed one with her hand. "Fake," she said. "You want to feel?"

I turned away from Claire and looked out at The Lake. People were splashing in the water. Some were lying on floats and paddling in rubber rafts. A metal rowboat in the center of the lake contained two men with a fishing poles. They were wearing straw hats.

"It's okay," Claire said. "I'm not going to say anything to your dad. You can test them. Then you'll know what fake ones feel like."

"I don't even know what a real one feels like."

Claire smiled and leaned toward me. I didn't want to touch them, but I also didn't want her to think I was afraid to. She pulled aside the bikini top as I reached up. I couldn't even fit an entire palm around one. I gave it a squeeze.

"Okay. That's enough." She pulled up her top and went back to reading.

We sat quietly for a while before Claire asked, "What're you thinking?"

"Are you and my Dad going to get married?"

She laughed. "No. I don't think so. I like your dad a lot, but I'm not sticking around this place. I'm getting out as soon as I have enough points."

"Where will you go?"

"Not sure. Maybe North Canada. Maybe Finland. Some place where nobody is constantly watching you." I felt hurt. I thought she liked me looking at her.

She must have read the expression on my face or heard my thoughts. She lightly touched my arm. "Not you, sweetie. You can watch all you want. I meant those cameras up there." She tilted her face toward the sky. "You can't see them, but they're everywhere."

It was nearing noon. You could tell because men all around The Lake were rising to their feet. I rose from the blanket and walked over to my rifle. I could sense Ellen's eyes on me, watching everything. I unlocked the trigger and carried it to The Lake. I stepped into the sticky, black foam, letting it seethe between each toe. Hundreds of men stood at the water's edge, guns and rifles in hand. Standing silent. Naked.

There was a loud cluster of explosive snaps as we fired into the air. My ears rang as though swarming with wasps. I felt woozy and staggered a bit. Ellen's hand rested on my back.

"Are you all right?"

She took hold of my arm. I tried to pull away, but she held tight.

"Here, let me help you."

A voice from somewhere, maybe inside my head, cried, *Security makes us free! Freedom makes us secure!*

"No," I said, "We have to get in. We need to get in now."

Ripples expanded from the shore as bodies lowered themselves beneath the lake's milky surface. I laid the rifle on the ground. Ellen clung tight to my arm. "Do we have to?" I didn't respond. I didn't want to draw any attention. She kept hold of my arm as I walked toward the water and followed me in.

Jody took a seat beside me on the refrigerator. We ate our pojay jerky in silence. The sky had lost some of its tawny-brown. It had become metallic blue, like the scoured underside of a steel pan. Maybe life was improving.

"So," Jody began after finishing the last bite of his jerky. He cleared his throat before continuing. "Things seem to be moving along nice for you and yer girlfriend."

"What are you talking about, Jody? Ellen? I told you, it's not like that."

"C'mon. C'mon. We all heard you took her to The Lake."

Maybe I shouldn't have been surprised Jody knew about Ellen and I going to The Lake. Nothing here goes unobserved by Skeye. Word travels faster than paramecium. Half the town knew Claire had passed her fertility test before Dad and I ever got word. The White Guard wasted no time leading her off to the Capital Venture Zone. All evening, we thought she was on the roof, tanning hides and hanging them to dry. But nearly everyone else knew she was at the Embarkation, awaiting passage to Topeka Canyon.

"She asked to go," I explained to Jody. "What was I supposed to say?"

"*No.*"

"I tried to discourage her from coming, but — "

"Hey, no need to make excuses, Ace. That's what she calls ya, ain't it? Believe me, I understand. A pretty thing like that. I'd be tempted to do something criminal for a face like hers."

"Let's not talk about her, Jody."

"Suit yourself, *Ace.*"

I hid out in the resource library on the basement floor most of the week, avoiding Ellen. I flipped through back catalogues, index files and Honor's Reports, trying to figure out how 3-Sector panels were produced in the old days. I was looking for a way to continue manufacturing the panels without columbite, which had been completely stripped from our side of the planet. Then I got sidetracked reading about the mine wars in Congo and the price-fixing of magnetic clouds across the Eastern Zone. Needless to say, I was not getting much real work accomplished.

Ellen finally caught up with me Friday while I was entering the parking dock.

"Hello stranger. We didn't get a chance to speak much this week."

She was dressed differently, more like other women at work. A knit palunke fell over her narrow hips. Algae leather slim joes covered her legs from waist to ankle. A grey-blue cowl hung around her neck, partially hiding her chin. I knew beneath the cowl there was a small bandage. People were gossiping about it, sharing giddy whispers of satisfaction, as if this blemish, or whatever it was, was something they gladly anticipated.

I clutched the keys to my shambles in my right hand, eager to get away.

"You have big plans for the weekend?"

"Oh, the usual," I replied. "Playing some motion cards, jelling some slot cones, relaxing in the salt mine…" I was careful not to mention The Lake gathering.

"Are you in a rush?" she asked. "I mean, do you have time to drive me home? I normally taxi my way back, but because of the black body convention at Fort Deed there's a forty-five minute wait for a driver."

Unable to think up a quick excuse, I found myself replying, "Sure. No problem."

I hadn't known where Ellen was living. I assumed it was Summerset Park. That's where they locate the new people in town — at least, the professionals. Street workers and cargo men are pretty much on their own and tend to settle into the shanty district close to the Expo Center.

Ellen directed me to turn left off the I-Beam onto Cavendish Road. "It's a little out of your way. I'm sorry."

"No worries," I responded, thinking, *Hell yes. This is way out of my way. What have I gotten into?*

Cavendish was barely a road any more. Fig weed, terra mites, and grange runoff had eroded large sections. I didn't know people still lived out this way. "It's quiet here," said Ellen, as if reading my thoughts once again. "I like open spaces, being able to view a big stretch of horizon. It's like staring out to sea."

We passed an abandoned education center with its playground still standing, though its swings were just chains dangling without seats. Beyond that was a decimated solar farm. Most of its steel-framed panels were missing or shattered into ground shards. Some were covered in layers of ash, foam disinfectant, decayed leaves and silt. Things moved in and out of the darkness beneath them, scurrying shadows.

"Can you slow down?" Ellen asked. I was already going pretty slow so as not to damage my shambles on the uneven pavement, but I downshifted to a crawl. Ellen peered toward the destroyed panels, as if searching for something.

"Ferals," I said, referring to the creatures beneath the rubble, hiding in the dark.

"I pass them every day on my way to work. There is one that sometimes races behind my cab. I try to get the drivers to stop, but they always refuse. No one wants to get near them."

"For good reason. They're loaded with all kinds of diseases and parasites. Every now and then you hear about an entire family that died from skulleye or stink needle and it turns out they got it from some feral burrowed beneath their home."

"But they weren't always like this." Ellen said, questioningly. "They had parents at one time, right? They were living in the community at some point, weren't they?"

"Can't say. Not sure where they come from. Can't get rid of them, though. The White Guards don't allow you to shoot them. And every time they're forced to the outskirts, beyond the Free Enterprise Zone, they eventually find their way back."

"You would think they could do something about them. I mean, not get rid of them, but rehabilitate them somehow."

"Oh, they've tried. Believe me. It's not easy. And we don't have the resources — " I abruptly slammed the brakes to avoid hitting a feral darting across the road. I heaved, as the seat strap dug into my waist. Ellen's head hit the dash.

"You okay?"

"Fine," she said. She peered out the window, trying to spot where the feral had run off to. "I think he was the one," she said. "There he is!" She pointed toward a pile of scrap metal ripe for scavenging. Buried within its dark hollow, you could see the little bugger's gleaming eyes. He was watching us.

Ellen reached for the door handle. I quickly yanked her arm away from the door. "Are you crazy!" I shouted. I hit the gas and peeled away.

"Sorry."

She leaned back and remained silent for a few minutes before speaking again. "I keep thinking he's probably the same age my brother would be right now."

I hadn't known Ellen had a brother. I didn't know anything about her family life, really. At The Lake we hadn't talked much. On the ride back, it was mostly her asking me questions about the town, my favorite ways to pass time and the visions that haunted me most.

"Well, lucky for you your brother isn't living in the wild. Where is he now, anyway?"

"I was told he was dead, along with my parents. They refused to be evacuated. This was in the Kettle Belt, before the silo leaks or, rather, shortly after the first one took place."

"That wasn't long ago," I said, thinking back. I started work at Revoun Engineering about that time. We were designing containing walls back then. I did a lot of work creating barriers to seal off the Kettle Belt and prevent silo contamination from spreading into the Drag Hills.

"But you got out okay, obviously."

"My parents told me to go with the White Guards. They promised to take us east to Topeka Canyon. My brother was too sick to travel, so they stayed with him."

Ellen was lucky. *Topeka Canyon!* What I wouldn't give to be living there.

"How did you end up here?" It wasn't the first time I'd asked. She'd given jokey answers in the past: *Just dumb luck! Rewards for a past life well lived! Blew in with the neon fog!* I hadn't pressed her. Some things are better left unknown. But now I needed to know. Who would leave Topeka Canyon for *this*?

"They were training me to be a White Guard, but I kept failing. That's when I was diagnosed with my *prosopagnosia*. They removed me from the institute, gave me a choice — work for Skeye News or come here."

"I would have worked for the news and stayed in Topeka Canyon."

"You don't seem to like it here."

"Do you? I mean, look at this place? No real plant life. The only thing green here is the autumn sky. And ferals everywhere. I bet they don't have ferals in Topeka Canyon?"

"No, they don't."

"Why leave?"

Ellen shrugged. She stared out the window, observing the rubble of bull-dozed homes and plowed over ammo supply shops. We drove for another ten minutes before she spoke again.

"Almost there," she said. "Up and to the left."

Her home was one of only several still standing in the area. Her *Joy Juice* colored house of freshly sanded pinewood stood out brightly amidst the dark terrain.

"It's small, but it's mine. I guess that's the tradeoff for living so far out of town."

I pulled into the driveway or, rather, what had once been a driveway. Now it was matted with torn chain metal and dead weeds. "Can I invite you inside, get you something to drink? I have real water!"

I wasn't so tempted. Mostly, when people say they have real water, they mean the stuff from Tapcore, semi-filtered drain pour, or Deed field condensation that still tastes of petrol.

"C'mon in, Ace. I have something to show you."

The house appeared even smaller on the inside. A decent-size living space, but a kitchen and bedroom no bigger than two *Sol Hapi* trailers. The basement, she said, was uninhabitable because of tar seepage. I gave a sniff but could not detect any tar smell, only a certain sweetness, which was probably from the jars of sycamore honey left open on the kitchen table.

"Is this what you wanted to show me?" I asked, indicating the honey.

"No. But you're welcome to take a jar. I get them from my neighbor, Bessie. She raises syc's in her backyard. I sometimes help with the milking. She gives me a jar to take home in return."

Ellen poured clear liquid from a plastic bucket on the counter into a tin cup. She handed the cup to me. "Here."

I took a sip. It was cool to the throat and swallowed easy.

"This is fresh water."

"The best water is the newest. My neighbor gets it from somewhere. She won't tell me where, though."

"People are secretive about that sort of thing."

Ellen turned her back to me, entered the living room and unlocked a small cabinet. Inside were three full shelves of books.

"They were here when I moved in. I guess nobody wanted them." She pulled out one of the volumes. "This is a book on leaves and flowers."

I walked over, took the book from Ellen, and flipped through the pages. *Irises. June Whistles. Bower Blooms. Sweet Cacti. Red lilies...*

She pulled out another volume. I recognized the cover. A naked man and women on horseback in a lush green forest. "My father's girlfriend Claire had that same book."

"It's my favorite," said Ellen. "Kahlad Aymen."

"I don't know who that is."

"Neither do I. I think he's Indian or something. This is an English translation. I wonder if it's even more beautiful in the original language." Ellen flipped open the pages and began to read at random.

> *Welcome, stranger, to this place.*
> *Where joy doth sit on every bough,*
> *Paleness flies from every face;*
> *We reap not what we do not sow.*

She left off reading with a frown and flipped to another page. "Love seeketh not itself to please, nor for itself hath any care, but for another gives its ease, and builds a Heaven in Hell's despair." She shut the book and thrust it at me. "Here, Ace. I want you to have it."

"I'm not much of a reader," I confessed.

"You will be after this."

I ended up staying at Ellen's that night. I'm not sure what they put in that sycamore honey, but it packs a punch.

Ellen rode with me into town. We didn't spot any ferals along the way, fortunately. They don't normally come out of hiding until early evening when the air has thinned and the sewers are flowing again.

We drove to Flat Rock to buy roach husks. Ellen uses them to shave her legs and remove dead tar mites from between her floorboards. I was also hoping to pick up some ammunition before heading to The Lake for the Saturday ritual.

With her cowl collar removed, I could clearly see the sore on Ellen's chin. The dab of epoxy placed on it did little to hide the raw flesh. Perhaps now she had a legitimate reason for going to The Lake and bathing with the rest of us.

When Ellen demurred my lake invitation, I was a little surprised.

"Let's do something else today. I hardly ever get out to see the sites. After Flat Rock, could we go for a walk in The Columns?"

The Columns were north of the city. It had once been an old forest. The trees died and blackened, but ash winds from the East turned them white, like tall marble columns extending up into the henna-brown cloud cover. My dad used to take me there with Claire for hikes and to buy sugared poultice from the vendors that park their truckettes just outside The Columns.

"This is like entering another world," said Ellen as we walked beneath the first row of tall, white columns. The air changed instantly. It was cooler and held the dull scent of clay. Compared to the air in town, it was like stepping atop a landfill of potpourri.

Since this was Lake Day, there was no one else around, except one old man preparing to leave The Columns. He eyed us suspiciously and kept his distance as he headed out toward the parking ring.

"There's a place off to the right where we'd go when I was a kid. It's a narrow rut between the trees. Dad said it was once a creek bed. You can follow it all the way into the Night Chambers."

"What are the Night Chambers?"

"They're way deep in The Columns. Light can't reach between the columns there. It's where people hid when the Corporals came through town, taking our phones, amulets, regenerators — anything valuable they could get their hands on."

"I thought the Corporals were sent to help people rebuild after the Red Rains?"

"Right. I don't mean to speak badly of the Corporals. I'm sorry. You won't tell anyone I said that, will you?"

Ellen laughed, then narrowed her brows in confusion. "Were people really afraid of them?"

"Let's keep walking."

Arrows carved into the columns marked the way. Some were numbered to show distance. We followed the arrows until coming upon a pile of roach husks someone had raked into a circle alongside the trail. Ellen lifted handful. "If I had known we'd find these, I wouldn't have had you drive me all the way to Flat Rock." She bit down on a husk.

"What are you doing?"

"They're edible. Didn't you know? They're full of amino acids. You could practically live off these things." She bit off a chunk and ground it between her molars. "Here. Try one."

"No thanks. I'm saving my appetite for pojay." *No one makes pojay, like Wesley makes pojay, 'cuz only Wesley's pojay is the best.*

Ellen emptied fistfuls of husks into her backpack. "They're not great tasting, I'll give you that. But not entirely awful."

Light grew dimmer the deeper we entered The Columns, yet the tall white columns always stood out in sharp contrast to their grey surroundings of brush and vines. Not far down the path we spotted a large black X carved into the surface of one column. "I remember this," I said. "I think the creek is just beyond here."

Ellen grabbed hold of my hand. I let her fingers lock over mine. Skeye could not peer between these closely gathered columns. And there was no one else here to notice or mind.

The creek was somewhat like I remembered it. A windy indentation running between columns, filled with rocks, tiny pebbles and grey powder. But, when I was a kid, the creek had been full of tiny bones and small skulls. I thought they were fish bones.

"There haven't been fish here in ages," Dad explained. "Those little skulls are dragon lizards. The bigger ones are mostly pests — forest rats, pole snakes, coon moths…"

Now they were only powder and tiny bone fragments, like grey confetti, tramped by the feet of so many recreational visitors. It crunched and shifted beneath us as we walked along the uneven creek basin. Our backpacks, full of pojay, root jerky and Tapcore 100, shifted side to side with every uneven step of the way.

I wanted to show Ellen the Mirror Pool, a shiny black surface that revealed reflections of faces without all their sores, blisters, pustules and what not. It had been my favorite place to go as a kid, the place where I first saw just how handsome Dad had once been and how beautiful Claire would have been if she'd grown up anywhere else but here.

"There!" I removed my hand from Ellen's and pointing down the trail. Black letters vertically carved upon a wide white columns read

M
I
R
R
O
R

P
O
O
L

We hurried over the rocks and bramble that littered our way, climbed up the creek bank and entered the circle of columns that surrounded the Mirror Pool. The pool was not as large as I remembered; three men laid head-to-foot could easily span the pool's circumference. Neither was it quite as opaque and reflective as I recalled. Flakes of mineral deposit sparkled just below its shiny black surface.

I knelt down to view my reflection. Faint light, pouring through The Columns, outlined the contour of my head. I could not distinguish any particular features, though, just the glow of my eyes. As a boy, I believed the pool removed all disfiguration. But, really, it had only hidden our unsightliness within its depths.

I watched Ellen's reflection enter the pool beside

mine. It was the same: a dark silhouette with glistening eyes.

"Our eyes are like stars," said Ellen. "It's like we're looking into a clear night sky and seeing our eyes amidst those shiny bits of starlight."

I was happy she could see this, at least — though it was not what I had hoped, that she might see the me I could have been if born in a different place and time.

I knelt until my knees grew sore and the voices in my head rose to a chorus of *The more points gained, the more freedom attained!*

Was it time to head back to the shambles?

"Should we move on?" Ellen asked. "Can we still reach the Night Chambers? Or is it too far?"

"We have time," I said. "We can go a bit further. I'm not sure, though, we can make it all the way to the Night Chambers."

Ellen's fingers curled within my own as we made our way toward the pitch black curtain in the distance. It did not seem far. We walked for nearly an hour, though, without ever quite reaching its threshold.

Ellen halted. "I see something." She pointed to where small lights appeared amidst distant columns. We hurried toward them.

The lights were nested within dead plant growth surrounding the base of several columns. Ellen pulled aside the desiccated vines and pressed a finger into the luminous goo. A clump detached, alighting the tip of her finger. She sniffed at it. "Smells like sea clams," she said. "Do you know what clams are?"

"Of course I do," I replied, though I'd never actually seen a real clam or had any idea what they smelled like.

"Smell it," she said. A glowing fingertip reached toward my face. As I leaned forward, she dabbed the goo to the tip of my nose. She backed away, gaping at my face, then burst out laughing.

I swiped a handful of goo off the column, lunged at Ellen and wiped it across her face before she could move away. It made her entire face glow.

Ellen wasted no time retaliating. She filled her hands with the luminous crud and rushed toward me. I grabbed her wrists, preventing her glowing fingers from contacting my skin. Her face was close to mine. Eyes glistening. Lips effulgent. Cheeks radiant with warm blood. A smile like a glowing, midsummer neon cloud.

"Oh, c'mon, Ace. Let me do you."

"No way."

"Please! I want to see."

I wondered if my skin, too, would glow like hers. But I was fearful what the goo might do to the sores, pustules and blemishes.

"Pretty please?"

I relaxed my grip and she freed her hands. The voice in my head said, *Liberty calls to those who glisten!* I gave in and let Ellen do me. "Don't get any in my mouth," I said, as her hands settled upon my skin and caressed my inflamed jowls.

Her hands smoothed goo across by brows and along my jaw, then over the lids of my eyeholes and around my lips. The smell was not unpleasant, just a bit odd. It had a soothing effect upon the ruptures and calmed the searing flames beneath the skin's surface.

Ellen stepped back to gaze at her handiwork. We both stood silently, watching each other's faces glow. What did she actually see amidst that iridescent slime?

"This is so cool," she whispered and gently pressed a finger to my cheek. "I can see your face now. My gosh, it's incredible."

She rose up on her toes. Our faces came together. Lips pressed, one to another. I could taste the goo, which was sweet and tingly. Ellen's tongue ran across my flayed lips. Her teeth gently clamped down, securing the lower fold, and gave a gentle tug before removing her face from mine.

We wiped our gooey fingers onto our jackovers, pantoons and trowlets. The glowing substance faded into the fabric. I raised a hand to wipe my face clean. "Don't," Ellen said. "Leave it. It's not uncomfortable, is it?" It wasn't. Not at all.

We walked deeper into the darkening columns. I wanted to see if we could truly reach the Night Chamber. The urge to turn back had receded. The voices in my head fell silent. If any cameras were watching, all they might have seen were two floating faces in the fading terrain, heading toward complete blackness.

"What would happen if we walked all the way through the Night Chamber?" asked Ellen. "What do you suppose is on the other side? Canada?"

I wasn't sure if she was joking. "It's vast," I replied. "I don't know anyone who's gone very deep."

"Let's see how far we can go. Maybe it's not as deep as people think."

"We need to get back before sunset."

"Why?"

I wasn't sure how to answer. "We just do."

"We could spend all night here, sleep on the ground if we get tired. There's no reason to return tonight. There's no reason to go back at all, is there? What if we kept walking all the way to Canada?"

"I can't tell if you're joking."

"When I lived in Topeka Canyon, they said, 'Don't leave. Skeye News isn't so bad. You have a life here other people would kill for. You don't have to tan hides or sell fresh organs. You can help The Reform, be remembered by generations to come.' I asked them, *What about the others?* 'You've been out there,' they said. 'You know what they're like. There's nothing we can do for them. We have to think of the future.'"

"And that's why you left? To help the rest of us?"

"No, Ace. I wasn't thinking in those terms. I was thinking about myself, mostly, about what I might actually want for my own children — if I ever have any. Children in Topeka Canyon were taught they were different, better than the rest. And that *their* children would grow up to be a beautiful new nation. I never believed that. You can't defer your hopes for another time, another generation or the generation after that. You have to make the best of what's here already."

Ellen smiled and placed her hands over her face, muting the glow. "You think I'm horribly simplistic, don't you?" she said through her palms.

I removed her hands so I could see her face once more. I had no idea what to say and there were no voices in my head to distract my mind and muffle my confusion with their words.

Ellen grabbed hold of my hands. "I'm not joking about Canada," she said. "We have plenty of pojay and water. And if we run out we'll gather more roach husks. I'm not tired. We could keep going. We could go on like this forever."

And so we did.

Second Nature

I'm a horse. I'm a horse. I have to keep reminding myself that. But, of course, a real horse wouldn't have to remind itself it's a horse. He's just a horse, regardless of what he thinks. Which leads me to believe, if I have to think I'm a horse I'm probably not much of a horse. The more I try to be a horse, the less certain I am about being a horse. I begin to question what it even means to be horse. And that just gets me nowhere. I need to stop thinking about it, brush off those pesky doubts. Just keep telling myself, over and over, I'm a horse! I'm a horse! until it becomes second nature.

The Right People

We were waiting for the right people, but the wrong people kept showing up. We'd go to the door thinking, *Finally, they're here*, open the door and be, like, *What the fuck? The wrong people.*

Just let them in, someone would insist. And so we would. *Sure. Wrong people, make yourselves at home.* Then we'd wait some more. And keep waiting. Sooner or later the right people were bound to arrive.

At first it was just us. Just us as long as I can remember. Us just trying to make do. But nothing seemed to work. We'd convene, discuss whatever situation was at hand, devise a plan, implement solutions and carry them out to varying degrees of success or failure. To be honest, more often failure than not.

Let's not panic, Fedorov would advise after every disaster. *Success comes at a price.* The Etruscans struggled for centuries to create a numeric system for Time. The Egyptians undertook dozens of pyramids before completing one that did not collapse into a heap during construction. The Wright Brothers dreamt up 129 different steam engine designs before building one strong enough to power a locomotive. And The Bee Gees recorded 17 version of Stayin' Alive before struck by the idea of recording in falsetto.

Blackburn corrected Fedorov, *The Wright Brothers invented the air-o-plane, not the steam train.*

Edwidge chimed in, *And they didn't use a steam engine. They used bicycle pedals.*

Shut up, Hedgepeth scolded. *Shut up, both of you.*

The bickering amongst ourselves started even before we first heard about the right people, back when we were hopelessly trying to make a go of it on our own. Then hope came along.

We first learned about the right people from magazine articles. Then saw their television specials. We monitored their blogs, social media accounts and message boards. Their thoughts and doings were endlessly blurbed and twitillated. They were out there. Dozens of them. Maybe hundreds. Possibly thousands. We sent up flares, beacons, pyres, semaphores, night howls. We spoke to people who spoke to people who knew people who could forward our invitations.

Indirect replies were conveyed. *They're coming. Be patient. They're on their way.*

This is why we were totally expecting the right people when the wrong people started to appear. The wrong people made themselves comfortable. They tried to blend right in. This created difficulties. You'd mistakenly offer something to a wrong person and everyone would be, like, *Whoa! Wait. That's totally a wrong person.*

Give it back, we'd insist. And the wrong person would be, like, *Too late, man. I already got my wrong-person germs all over it. Ha ha!*

There were a lot of them, these wrong people. And they kept coming, taking up space. We were going to need more room for when the right people showed up. Long discussions were held about getting rid of the wrong people, how to go about it, what to say, who gets their stuff when they're gone. We spent way too much time talking about it and by the time anyone was ready to do anything, many of the wrong people had already started hooking up with some of us, even conceiving our future children and opening startup juice bars and cafes.

Now what? We wondered. *Does this make them one of us or are they still the wrong people?*

Once a wrong person, always a wrong person, Blackburn would repeat over and over.

Put it on a bumper sticker, dude, said Ryland.

Blackburn's maxim sounded plainly wrong to many of us. Didn't everyone have the potential to change, to make something new of themselves? Weren't we awaiting the right people for that very purpose, to help us evolve, improve our lot in life. Weren't we all hoping for a little of that rightness to rub off on us?

Maybe they're not coming, said Hedgepeth, growing distressed. *If they were, they'd be here by now.*

Maybe they were here already, or close by, said Blackburn. *And they saw all these damn wrong people and were, like,* Fuck this. We're not going anywhere near some wrong people sort of place. *So they turned and high-tailed it back home.*

Could that have happened? Could they really have mistaken us for wrong people? I hope not. There are plenty of wrong people among us, but we are clearly different. We are the sort of people who have the sheer will and fortitude to wait things out. We are unwavering, unyielding, sober and pragmatic. We are the ones who believe, despite all uncertainty, that the right people will come. Such conviction is etched in our countenance, carried in our bearing and must surely be apparent from afar.

When they finally arrive — and they will arrive — the right people will appraise us and plainly discern those of us *here first* from the newly arrived wrong people. They will be, like, *Brothers! Sisters! So good to be with you all at last*, and hold us tight to their rightly bosoms.

All we need do is wait. Keep on *keeping on*. Hope more wrong people do not find their way to our door. Bear with those already here, if we must, but never too embracingly. Above all, never lose heart — not that it's in our nature to do anything else. Waiting is in our blood. It's what keeps us going and sustains our hope, even as the days grow darker and our fields grow drier, and the wrong people persist in coming, as if this were the right place for them.

Phantom Limb

Three feet of water in the hold and rising. Life rafts at the ready. Mayday response received by patrol boat six nautical miles southeast. Monkeys scrambling up the control tower, leaping along cables spanning bow to stern. Wake from the pirate's cutter subsiding as the ship speeds toward the horizon. Machine guns cracking rounds in the distance. Heather turns to me and says, "This is probably not the best time, but I want you to know I'm not pregnant."

"Not the best time," I say. "Help me get that monkey." I point toward a silver-haired vervet clinging to a wall-mount fire extinguisher. "You keep his attention." I circle wide, moving close behind, before stumbling over some ropes lying in a puddle of rainwater, mixed with the blood and urine of the dead Moroccan.

When I come to, I am lying on a damp canvas stretcher, rain splashing my face and hair. It drips into my eyes and over the sides of my neck, collecting beneath me. A compressed voice crackles through a radio speaker. "Kaplich Bay ready with CG unit...Roger...We stand by."

A woman speaks. "There were monkeys. Did you see them?"

The stretcher bangs against a metal rail. "*Gard-a-vous!*" shouts a man's voice.

My group, the World Animal Liberation Fund (WALF), hoped to raise 48,000 US dollars to free 39 monkeys from brutal captivity in Kenya. In October last year, I came across an article in the German newspaper *Die Zeit* about monkeys being trained by Kenyan military to fight Al-Shabaab. The article included photos of their trainer flailing a section of rubber hose. I contacted Harvard zoologist, Dr. Anthony Petrov, who confirmed militaries around the world have used monkeys in battle, including the US. "But these programs have had little success," he told me in our Skype interview. "Monkeys are fairly unpredictable. They challenge authority more often than human soldiers. I'd be skeptical of anyone claiming they're used in battle. What's more likely, they're being used to clear land mines."

"You mean, setting them off?"

"That's right. *Ka boom.*"

I wrote an article, published it in our organization's monthly newsletter. It was picked up by over 14 online publications, including *The Huffington Post*. This led to an extremely successful fundraiser. We exceeded our goal by an additional 30K. By then, however, we had a far more complicated mission than originally planned.

"How's your head?" Heather asks. I'm lying on a metal cot inside some ship cabin. It smells of feces and tobacco. The cot is dry, but my shirt and pants are damp.

There is a wool blanket covering me.

"I'm okay," I say. I try to pull off the blanket with my good arm. Heather pulls it back over me.

"Rest a moment. The ship's captain is coming to take a look at you."

"You can take a look, can't you? You're the medical expert."

"I'm a researcher, not a doctor. I can only look at blood through a microscope. Otherwise, I get woozy."

"Are you positive you're not pregnant?"

"Positive."

Captain Freddy lowers his head as he enters the cabin. He's a tall, dark-skinned man. Young for a captain, though hard to say exactly how young. He wears a short-sleeve green polo shirt and black beret angled over his broad face. He is either humming or making a small propeller noise with his lips.

"Let's see what we got here," he says, after introducing himself. He pulls a small stool beside my cot and rips into my shirt sleeve with a pocket knife. He says not to worry. He has medical training. Attended medical school in Le Havre, France for six months. "Poco," he calls to a man standing outside the cabin door. "Bring me my kit."

Freddy cautiously tears apart my damp sleeve trying to get at the wound. "Smile," he says as I flinch. "I see much worse."

Poco returns and hands Freddy a plastic tackle box. Inside are medical supplies. Freddy takes out a pair of scissors, a roll of gauze, a bottle of hydrogen peroxide and a deck of playing cards. "Tell me your name," he says, as he scissors the sleeve away from my arm.

"Paul," I say. "Paul David."

"Which one? Paul or David? You not so sure?" He grins.

"It's Paul. David is my surname."

"Ah! Okay, man." He chuckles as he presses some peroxide-soaked gauze onto the wound above my elbow. "Ya. It sting, no? You have nice bite here. This need stitching." He turns to Heather. "You okay? Maybe you sit down."

Heather probably thought I was lying when I said we didn't need protection. Donna, my ex, and I had tried for nearly four years to conceive. Her tests were fine. Mine came back *not so* fine. I was diagnosed with a condition that hurts to even pronounce — chronic hypogonadotropic adenohypophsis hypopituitarism — which, simply put, is some sort of incurable hormonal deficiency.

Heather had missed her second period in two months. And the pregnancy test turned out positive. A bit of a miracle, I thought. But not quite what either Heather or I were planning. We'd known each other only a few months. She was overwhelmed with finishing her studies, preparing her dissertation *and* working part time at the IU Pathology Lab. I was still sorting through my apartment, finding things Donna had left behind, throwing them out or giving them away. Relationship, commitment, family — these were things Heather and I were not yet prepared for.

"It's not supposed to look like this," Heather says, as she examines my arm back home in Indiana. It has been five days since we'd returned to Champaign. Dr. Kremeschi at the campus Christie Clinic undid Freddy's sloppy stitches, cleaned the wound, and resewed everything. He wrote a prescription for antibiotics and codeine, and sent me home.

Heather fights her queasiness while further unraveling the bandage. There are blue and yellow streaks extending from the red skin around the suture. I assure her it's okay. The antibiotics will soon kick in.

Heather winds a fresh bandage around my arm and secures it with metal fasteners. Resting her head against my shoulder, she says, "Not one monkey." "Not one," I repeat. In the end, despite all our effort, we hadn't managed to save a single monkey.

I return to Dr. Kremeschi's office twice over the next four weeks. Each time he cleans the wound, he prescribes a stronger antibiotic. On my third visit, his eyes widen as he peers beneath the bandage. He speaks slowly, in an exaggerated casualness that sounds false to my ears.

"It might be a good idea for one of my colleagues to take a look."

He leaves the room. I'm expecting him to return with another doctor. Instead, he returns with a prescription pad. "You okay to drive?" he asks. He tears off the paper and hands it to me. It contains a name and address. "Take 74 east to Saint Joseph's Medical Center. Do you know it? Ask for Dr. Alasdair Plaxton. He'll be expecting you."

"Right now?" asks Heather.

"Yes. No sense waiting on this any longer."

I'm driving 74 past Walmart and AutoZone, trying to figure out what exactly the doctor means by *waiting on this*. Waiting on what? A second opinion? Something better than stitches? Each time I shift lanes, a stabbing pain shoots up my arm and into my armpit. I settle into the right lane and stay there until the Saint Joseph's turn off.

"Hold on," I say. "I'm not losing an arm over a monkey bite."

Heather leans in and presses her lips to my forehead. She pulls back my hair, damp with sweat, and runs her small fingers through the damp curls. "It doesn't make sense," I say. "Shouldn't we talk to another doctor? It was just a stupid bite, for chrissake."

A nurse draws a syringe full of blood. She gives me an injection from a separate needle. Dr. Plaxton says I'm on the strongest antibiotics they have. "If this doesn't work we'll have to take other measures." Specifically, he says. "We'll have to consider transhumeral amputation. That's the only sure way to prevent the infection from spreading past the arm and endangering the heart. But let's hope it doesn't get to that."

Heather takes my finger in her hand and gives it a shake. "It's okay, babe," she says. "Get some rest. I'm sure it will be much better in the morning."

They keep me in the hospital overnight. In the morning, things appear worse. "No breakfast for you," says Dr. Plaxton. "You're scheduled for surgery at noon."

First thing I did was sell the blue Volkswagen Beetle and buy a used Honda with automatic transmission. Then I ordered a special computer keyboard designed for one-handed typing.

I am quickly adapting. My left hand cursive is legible and improving in speed. Occasionally, I still try reaching for something with my right arm before realizing my mistake. The most difficult things are the simplest, like getting dressed. But I've developed strategies for slipping into shirts, pulling up socks and clasping belt buckles. My therapist is impressed with my progress, but still keeps trying to push anti-depressants on me.

Once I could pretty much navigate life on my own, Heather stopped fretting and began focusing on her studies again. Though she is now on birth control, we see each other less. We only sleep together occasionally. Our relationship has gone back to being casual and ambiguous. It's hard to say whether we're drifting apart or just drifting along.

I've gotten back to my journalism work, producing a few short articles over the past couple months. I type slowly, but my one-handed technique is improving. I've also been helping with some of the WALF work. Normally Veronica Lee handles grant writing, but it's a lot of work for one person and we have dozens of grants to submit before year end. Veronica and I now meet a couple times a week at the Cafe Kopi to use their wifi.

"We got an email from Kenya," says Veronica. I set the soy latte beside her laptop and take a seat across the table.

"What's up?"

"They found one of the monkeys."

"You're kidding."

"It's from a warden at the Kenyan Wildlife Service. Felix Mwangangi. Felix says they call the monkey Jonah. He's living at the Malindi Marine Sanctuary. An excursion boat found him drifting on top a transport crate. He was severely dehydrated. He's recovered now. Here's a picture." Veronica turns her laptop to show me the photo. The monkey's teeth fill half the screen, its eyes glowing red from the camera flash.

Even Heather — especially Heather — is against the idea of me going to Kenya to finish the job and bring the surviving monkey home to its native India. "You're being too impulsive. Wait a year. If you still think it's a good idea, then go."

The board refuses to allocate any money for my return to Kenya, even though there is 70K in funds we haven't touched. My therapist has no objection. "If you feel up to it," she says. "Why not?" *Why not.* There are probably a dozen reasons why not. Most of them Heather has already spelt out for me. But I feel compelled, as if returning the monkey will restore some balance to the universe. Or, at least, my own existence.

I call Felix from the Bogart American Bar in Malindi. He tells me to meet him at the KWS (Kenyan Wildlife Sanctuary) office. "It is in the park near the beach," he says. "Not far. I will be waiting for you."

I head on foot toward the coastline, but cannot figure out whether to go north or south. I am the only white man out walking. Two boys run to greet me. "Hello! Hello! Where are you from?"

They offer to take me to the sanctuary. They know the quick way. We hurry through a residential area, rows of small, cinder block homes with corrugated metal rooftops. We pass a complex of resort buildings, two-story villas with thatched roofs, bay windows and green lawns surrounded by iron fences.

The boys ask the same questions over and over. I give them different answers. "Where you from? America?! Oh! Oh! You know LeBron James!" The other boy elbows him in the ribs. "Where are you from? Kathmandu?! Is that a real place?"

"Do you know Tiger Woods?"

"Michael Jackson!" shouts his companion and slaps his friend on the butt. They chase each other toward the empty parking lot. They stop halfway across and wait for me to catch up.

"You want to see dolphins? We know a very good boat. Captain, Mr. T. He take you to the best places, past Mosquito Bay. Turtles. Dolphins. Sharks. Whatever you want to see."

"I'm here to see a man about a monkey," I say.

"A monkey!" they scream in unison. "We know a very good monkey." The second boy hops on the first boy's back. The first boy pretends he is being attacked, spinning around in circles and flailing his arms.

"This is a special monkey," I say, catching up to them. "How much further to the Wildlife Sanctuary office?"

"It is there." One boy points to a small cinder block structure painted white with blue elephants and the letters KWS on its side.

The tiny building has a wood door and a large window facing the ocean. There is no glass on the window, only a metal latch and a wooden shutter hanging beneath it. Several photocopied flyers are tacked to the shutter. One of a missing child. One for sailing classes. Another for a Benga music festival. On a shelf inside the window are racks of brochures for resort hotels, boat excursions, safaris and wild game restaurants. The door opens and a man in a military-style, button-down shirt and khakis steps outside.

"Are you Mr. David?"

"Paul," I say, shaking his hand. "You must be Felix."

"Sorry, I was on my way to meet you and I had a phone call. Come, I show you our little friend."

Felix leads me to the beach. The sand is white and mixed with ground coral, metal bottle caps and cigarette filters. The palm leaves signal to the right from the strong breeze. Only a few people are lying out or splashing in the waves. They look more like local teenagers, not tourists. Two hundred yards further along the beach appear wooden boats in many bright colors. Waves rock them side to side. Their canopies rustle in the breeze. Several men are standing on shore talking and sharing cigarettes.

The two boys had been keeping a cautious distance but, upon seeing us heading toward the boats, they run up beside me. "We will show you the best boat ride," says one. "I know where is giant monster crab, big as this," He holds his arms out impossibly wide. His friend makes claws with his hands and pinches the other boy. They scuffle, slapping and twisting each other's skinny arms. Felix laughs.

When we near the boats, the boys run ahead shouting *Zumba!* A monkey, perched on the stern of one boat, turns in our direction. He rises to his feet as the boys approach. He leaps away before they can grab him.

"That's Jonah," says Felix. "But sometimes they call him Zumba. He will answer to either name."

When we reach the boats, Jonah is clapping his hands and waiting for the boys to feed him something. "You want banana, Zumby?"

One of the men hands the boys a banana to feed the monkey. He observes Felix and I walking toward him and waits for us.

"Aziz, this is the American I told you about."

Jonah climbs onto Aziz's shoulders. He rests his tiny paws on Aziz's bald head, his jaw still chewing away at a section of banana.

"You should have seen Jonah when I find him. I think, he is not going to make it. But look at him now." Aziz lifts the monkey off his shoulders. "He is almost fat!"

He holds Jonah out at arm's length. Jonah springs toward me. I raise my arm to catch him, but there is no need. He has me by the neck and shoulder, his legs wrapped around my waist. He moves one paw toward my face, touches my jaw and looks into my eyes. He grins. His lips separate revealing many little white teeth crammed together in his mouth. Then he leaps toward the boys, pleading for more banana.

Felix, having carried out introductions, wishes me well and heads back to mind the KWS office.

I hire Aziz to take myself and the two boys on a boat excursion to view the marine park and sanctuary. Jonah balances on the edge of the boat, steadying himself with one of the metal canopy poles. He is playing tour guide, perhaps imitating the gestures Aziz has repeatedly performed. Occasionally his small paw points toward something beneath the water or in the distance.

Look! There is a turtle, he appears to be saying. Then, pointing toward the shore: *There! Limestone caves. In the evening bats flow from them like black smoke.* He points right beneath the boat and makes a *wooting* noise, like a deranged owl.

The boys rock the boat as they scamper toward Jonah. They lean over the side. Sunlight moves straight through the surface, casting shadows upon the sandy bottom. They point to the wreckage of an old sailing ship. Its side is cracked open revealing a hull of sand and old glass bottles.

"A boat!" says one boy.

"Pirate ship," says the other.

Aziz brings the excursion boat ashore on a nearby islands. Here the beach is pristine with blinding white sand. The surrounding water is turquoise. Schools of small fish glide like cloud shadows beneath the surface. The boys, in their plastic sandals, splash along the shoreline. They chase red crabs. When the crabs turn to attack, the boys scamper away from their snapping claws.

Aziz lights a cigarette and offers me one. I decline, but Jonah raises a paw toward Aziz as if expecting one for himself. "He sometimes think he is little man," says Aziz. "He is very hairy, no? Hairy for even a monkey."

Aziz kicks some sand toward Jonah. The monkey leaps away and sets his dark eyes upon me.

"He's not from around here," I say. "He's from the north of India where it's not quite so warm."

"Ya. Ya. I know," says Aziz. "Felix tell me this. You want to bring him home, yes? Return him to his people." A puff of smoke comes out of Aziz's nostrils as he chuckles. "Sorry," he says. "He is a good monkey, but he is a monkey." He reaches into the boat for an empty Pepsi bottle and drops his cigarette butt inside. "Do what you like, though. I must piss. I will be right back." He walks toward a trail and disappears behind the mangroves.

I walk along the beach. The wet sand is lined with bird tracks and scattered with the open shells of razor clams and scallops. The waves are calm here. Across the water, there is another, smaller island with no trees, just tall grass and a few heron standing tall-legged on the sand. Past that island is a jetty with limestone cliffs. Beyond them, large ocean waves break against boulders, spray bursting in all directions.

A flock of birds, maybe pelicans, comes toward us from the North, their large wings fold and span with an instinctive allelomimesis that prevents them from colliding. As I gaze up at the flock, I sense something holding my fingers, squeezing and pulling on them. When I look down, there is Jonah, a paw raised as if holding on, though there is no hand, only a sensation of what should have been there.

Microwaves

Where I come from, the doctors not only diagnose and treat illness, but they also predict your future. Their training is extensive. It often begins in childhood when they are given an apprenticeship with a local doctor. At first, they may only be asked to perform menial tasks — cleaning, serving meals, gathering medicinal plants from the forest or running to the store to buy cigarettes. But, over time, the apprentice gains knowledge of the doctor's work and eventually assists in some of the more complicated treatments and divinations.

My older brother, Anush, was preparing to become a doctor, so I was able to observe first-hand how busy these young apprentices were kept. Unfortunately, Anush was hit by a military vehicle while crossing the street to buy cigarettes and did not survive his injuries — just as the doctor had foreseen. My parents had wanted me to follow in Anush's footsteps. But, to be honest, I was fearful of our local doctor and the sight of amputated limbs always makes me queasy.

One day, however, I was asked to assist the doctor with a non-medical emergency. He had recently acquired a microwave oven and did not know how to set the clock. Most people in our village have coal ovens, if they even have ovens, and hardly any ever heard of a *microwave*. But I had spent that summer in the capital visiting cousins and had the great opportunity to use their microwave oven to melt goat cheese onto a head of broccoli. My parents thought this knowledge might be useful to the doctor and offered him my assistance.

The doctor owned the nicest and largest home in our village. Situated on the hillside, it had a view of our entire valley. On a clear day you could see past the hills, straight to the distant, ever-rising sea. He lived on the second floor, while the first floor was devoted entirely to his medical practice and prognostication work.

The doctor knew I was coming. He stood by the door, ready to greet me. "Come in, child," he said, hurrying me inside. He ushered me through the workroom. Shelves along one wall were full of glass jars containing oils and powders. Plant roots, stems and leaves were strewn upon countertops. Anatomical drawings were taped over doors and cupboards. An AM/FM radio receiver sat upon a standing tray, surrounded by corn husk figurines, melted candles and small bones.

"Don't dawdle," he said, pulling me toward the staircase. "You have work to do."

The microwave was, fortunately for me, nearly identical to the one my cousins owned. Its clock, though smaller, worked in a similar manner and could be reset and changed by simultaneously holding down the plus and minus buttons.

"How did you do that?" asked the doctor.

"You see these two buttons? You press them both, then when the light blinks you double tap the plus button to show the year, then hold the minus button to —
"

"Never mind! Never mind! I will never understand this machine."

In gratitude for setting the time on his microwave, the doctor prepared a meal of hassock and squid peas for me. He left me alone in the kitchen while I ate. I stabbed at the ruby squid peas while watching the numbers on the microwave clock change every 60 seconds. After 11 minutes, the doctor returned from smoking his cigarettes on the balcony.

"I can see you are a clever child," he said, standing behind me. "Would you like to become my assistant?" I thought of what had happened to my brother, Anush. I worried what would happen if the doctor foretold my future. Would it change my life? Would knowing the future make it inevitable?

The numbers on the clock moved once again. It was an entirely new set of numbers. Just like that, time had completely flipped. I knew I could change it back, something the doctor did not know. A microwave can move time forward and backwards. I thought of my brother, Anush. What if I turned back the time to the moment before he was killed? Could I convince Anush to disobey the doctor and not run to the store for more cigarettes? Or would I find myself reliving the same series of events, powerless to stop them? Could I use the microwave to weave a completely different future into being? Would undoing the given flow of time anger the gods, delight them, completely ruin a perfectly good, if somewhat outdated, microwave?

The doctor was waiting for my answer. "Speak up. I'm offering you a great opportunity. Not just anyone gets to work for a village doctor, especially one as well-connected as I am. What are you staring at? Are you daft?"

I kept my eyes on the microwave. I did not respond. I did not need to. Any village doctor worthy of his bone saw, prayer beads and feather talismans could have foreseen my answer.

Conference

No one knew what took place in the conference room. The walls were granulated cork and insulated to absorb sound. There were no interior windows, just a solid, oak door. They'd enter — the seven, sometimes eight of them — and immediately close themselves inside. Meetings occupied three to five hours at a stretch. Occasionally Shakina would stand outside the entrance, bearing food deliveries or trays of coffee, tea and bottled water. Sometimes one participant or another would leave, hurry down the hall to the toilets, then return along the main corridor, passing us *slowly*, scrutinizing our monitors, workstations, award plaques, inspiration boards and business casual attire.

I was fairly certain they were talking about us in there.

When leaving the conference room, you could often detect a vague sense of relief in their manner and expressions, as if something had been partially resolved, or some consensus reached. They would loiter within the office a short while — collecting jackets, returning cups and saucers to the kitchenette, washing up in the restroom — before leaving. Through the glass wall at the reception area you could observe them crowd into the elevator. Out the East-facing windows, you could peer through the vertical blinds and watch them stride along the boxwood hedges toward the side parking. They'd say a few words of departure to one another, get into their black sedans, and drive off.

By most accounts, they appeared to be typical professionals — men in tailored suits and solid ties, women in pressed slacks with jewellery-draped sweaters and blouses. But little things seemed off. The eyes, for example. They rarely blinked or raised a brow. Perhaps symptoms of Botox. Or maybe part of their training. Who knows? Then there was the way they walked, as if measuring each stride. Hands hung low at their sides. Laughter when it happened — and it happened rarely — sounded rehearsed. Their presence, simply, made us all a tad uncomfortable.

We knew little about them, only that they outranked us in some unspecified way. They would come and go as they pleased, occupying our conference room, drinking our best teas. Their self-assured bearing was an annoyance, a slight. So, too, was their aloof manner toward us wee underlings, we who toiled day-in and day-out before our terminals, ogling metrics, data analytics, cross-functional feedback, pattern recognition, sequence labels and correlation clusters.

I wanted to know who they were and what they did, but Jennifer said it was best to keep quiet and *mind our own bee's wax*.

"I'm just curious, Jen. It's human nature to want to know. We're 'wired to inquire,' as the expression goes."

"Get over it, Andy. You've nothing to gain and everything to lose."

I don't recall when the plan to surreptitiously record the conference room first came to mind. The thought was there long before I was willing or able to act upon it. I debated the idea, over and over, uncertain it was worth the risk. If caught it could mean losing my position at the Institute. It would also be plain embarrassing. Who does such a thing? It's creepy, I know. Hiding microphones. Planting cameras. Spying through windows. It's paranoid behavior. I'm not that sort of person. You can check my files with HR. I score well within blue on the Caliper profile, just above standard on the Madstone Multiphasic Personality Inventory and a solid 120 on the Kihlstrome Scale, making me practically as normal and level-headed as they come.

Jennifer's warning stuck in my head. *Nothing to gain, everything to lose.* I felt she knew more than was letting on. I coaxed her to elaborate, but she poopooed me. "It's not a big deal," she said later. There were legal issues involved, that's all she knew. *Nothing we need be concerned about.*

"The rest of us barely notice them," she added. "It's strange, if you ask me, that you bother to keep track of changes among their members. Some turnover is not unusual."

"Not in our department," I pointed out. "No one ever leaves here." Out the corner of my eye I caught Bryan staring, listening in. When I turned, he looked away, pretending to be deeply engrossed in the new paper shredder's operation and safety manual.

It frustrated me no one else cared to know more. If the conference group was working on policy changes, or toward restructuring programs, procedures and positions within the institute, we all had a right to know. But Jennifer grew increasingly irked with my concerns. Others responded with shrugs, sighs, feigned disinterest. I eventually dropped the subject, not wanting to make more waves than I could capably navigate during our current climate of social and economic uncertainty.

On the radio, driving to and from the Institute, the news grew exponentially bleaker. The economy dipped. Spending sagged. Employment dried to a fiscal pumice leaving large sectors fully unemployed. Crops fried beneath caustic solar flares. Farms and valleys collapsed to dust and dross. Populations migrated north. Super-bugs propagated. Explosions rocked and roiled the border states. Security patrols marched and menaced the citizenry. Dissidents ceased bothering to protest all the CCTV monitoring, the unwarranted home inspections, and the incessant mandatory medical checks that encumbered our daily lives.

Had any of that to do with the notable uptick in conference meetings? They began gathering more frequently — twice, sometimes three times, weekly. No longer did they appear to resolvedly end their discussions. The conferees withdrew from the room with pursed lips and waxen eyes. They wordlessly left the building, sometimes not even bothering to rinse their plates, spoons and mugs.

This concerned me. As it should have concerned us all. Whatever was happening in the conference room did not look good. Did my colleagues care? Not one iota. They buried their heads in work, pretending these conferences had nothing to do with them. No curiosity. No initiative. No wonder the Institute was failing.

I set the bedroom alarm ninety minutes earlier than usual. My wife, somnambulantly, threw back the covers, ready to rise. "It's only six," I whispered. "Go back to slumberland. I'm getting an early start." She rolled onto her side without question and immediately began to lightly respire. I had told her nothing about my plan. This was something she did not need to be involved in given the sensitivity of her own work and career.

It was still dark out as I drove along the quiet parkway. I pulled into the empty office lot and parked in back. It began to drizzle as I walked toward the front door. It were locked, as expected — too early for Stanislav to be working the reception desk. I fumbled with my keys. We all had keys for working after hours. The Institute, with its compulsive frugality, employed no overnight guards to let anyone in or out after hours.

I quietly entered the spacious lobby of green marble, smoke-tinted glass and chrome. I peered behind the reception console to see if the camera monitors were recording. The ten small screens were blank. All they contained were reflections — my hands, my face, the chrome frames of my eyeglasses.

On the wall behind the console hung a square metal plaque. It read, *These premises secured by Skeye Lynx Surveillance.* I doubted this old security system still worked, or if the videos were ever properly saved and archived. Often just the threat of surveillance is enough to affect people's behavior. That's how it works with our call centers in Hattiesburg and Ypsilanti. Just the suggestion of monitoring is enough to spike response from the worker's amygdala, keeping them fully vigilant and attentive to calls.

This drives my wife crazy. She says warning signs without functional surveillance undermines the whole idea of security. True, long-term security, she says, is not something you can fake. But her career as a security analyst and troubleshooter, perhaps, biases her judgement against such cost-saving work-arounds.

It was strange seeing the office without people. It was like a film set of an office, not an actual office. A pretend office. A Potemkin workplace. I took off my coat, left it at my workstation, and walked to the far end of the building. I hesitated before the conference room doorway. Was I actually doing this?

I had only ever seen the conference room through the doorway at a distance, so I wasn't entirely sure what to find. There was not much to it, actually. Simply a long, white table surrounded by a dozen bone-white, high-backed, swivel chairs. The exterior wall was tinted glass from floor to ceiling, with black vertical blinds. It had no proper view. The neighboring office tower loomed close, windowless and uniformly concrete. The room's floor was overlaid in dark-lavender, pile carpeting. The ceiling was composed of white partition, with inset halogen bulbs. At one end of the conference room were empty, low-rise shelving units and a 56-inch, wall-mounted display monitor. At the other end hung a silver-framed art print — a watercolor abstraction of either an aroused vagina or the washed-ashore corpse of a pink dolphin. Your basic conference room, really.

I took the Diasonic DDR recorder out of my shoulder bag, along with a roll of black duct tape. The recorder was programmed to run continuously from early Monday morning through Friday night. I'd replaced the original SDI card with a larger, 32 gigabyte storage card. Maximum recording time: 120 hours. I turned on the recorder and set the level to 10. I crawled under the table and secured the device below with two strips of tape.

As I hurried out of the room, I reflected on what I had just done. I was both amused and shocked. It was all rather foolish of me, wasn't it? I am no James Bond and the conference room is not some North Korean missile silo or clandestine Zambian terrorist enclave. What did I hope to expose but my own foolishness?

I arrived each morning that week with a sense of foreboding. I half expected to encounter investigators dusting the conference room for prints. Maybe a uniformed guard waiting at my workstation or a police investigator snooping through my files.

Nothing like that happened, though. The following days proceeded as usual. A conference convened on Tuesday for three hours. A second one on Thursday for four.

In my observation notes, I refer to one of the conferees as Elvira. She has been with the group for several months. She arrives before the rest. She is tall, with long black hair parted in the middle. Shakira hands her the room sign-in log. Elvira writes the time and initials the entry before handing back the clipboard.

Elvira was often followed by a bald guy. I refer to him in my notes as *Baldy*. I have nomenclature for them all. The tweedy one is *Professor*. The short one with the high-pitched laugh, *Paul Simon*. The heavy-set one, *Tubby*. The tall, skinny one *Legs*. The Pakistani, *Pako*. And so on.

The following Saturday, I retrieved my recorder with no incident. Back home, I transferred the file from SDI card to laptop. I struggled with the unintuitive audio software I'd recently installed, referring to online tutorials for instruction. Eventually, I managed to get the recording to sound through my headphones.

There was not much to hear, only the drone of the AC unit. I turned up the volume and applied a noise gate. This allowed me to discern a passing jet engine and the squeaky chassis of a truck turning on the street below. I watched for any dramatic upticks in amplitude, as I scrolled further along the audio track.

Then, nearly fifteen hours in, the sound wave began to leap like a demon rollercoaster. I let it play. A forceful bray, like a mighty centaur, resounded in my ears. After that: a long hiss, like a large snake or a punctured air mattress. Then silence again. I navigated the indicator further along, until reaching another frenetic cluster of amplitude waves, and listened: a growling noise, a roar, a lunge and crash. It was like being trapped in a cage with a raging beast. As the sound diminished in volume, it transformed, settling into the familiar hum of a vacuum cleaner, followed by ten minutes of a damp cloth rubbing against a hard surface. Then liquid squirting. A woman clearing her throat. Chair casters rolling over carpet. A sneeze and sniffle. Then complete silence after the closing of a door.

I scrolled ahead on the timeline. The sound wave was practically a flat line. It wasn't until 180 minutes into the recording that I noticed another substantial uptick. I clicked the stop button, rewound and listened.

They each entered the room without any audible greeting. Perhaps they smiled, nodded heads, waved hello, signalled recognition in some unspoken form. Briefcases unclasped. Straps unfastened. Laptops banged the formica table top. Chair backs creaked on metal hinges. Seat cushions sighed. Not a word was spoken. They seemed to be working independently. *Tappet-y-taps* on keyboards. Sporadic mouse clicks. A mucus cough. Some paper shuffling. Clearing throats. Indiscernible mumbling. The scratch of a pen nib.

The first words spoken referred to hunger and where to order lunch. They could not agree. Three wanted Golden Dragon. Two preferred Three Kings Pizza. One suggested sushi. Another: sub sandwiches. One of the Golden Dragons switched to Three Kings. The one who'd wanted sushi switched to sandwiches on condition they order from Shelly's Deli. Momentum swung toward Shelly's Deli. Shelly's Deli and Three Kings battled it out for an extraordinary six minutes before Shelly's eventually ruled the day. Pako, the man with the Pakistani accent, placed the order over his cell phone.

The ordering process was followed by a lengthy discussions on corned beef, pastrami, heart disease, sourdough and pickles. Conversation ebbed and flowed for thirty-odd minutes, until Shakina knocked and entered with their delivery bags. Their eating and digesting was surprisingly, and disturbingly, quite audible. After lunch, there was a chorus of crinkling wax wrappers, paper bags and cardboard containers. A crescendo of straw slurps and gaseous burps. "Excuse me," whispered one lady.

I skipped around, hoping to find a substantive conversation, but there was only random comments having little to do with one another, and nothing to do with the Institute. Either their work was too technical to be communicated audibly, or it was too secretive to be spoken out loud, even within the confines of the conference room.

I sensed I was being watched. Out the corner of my eye, I caught a glimpse of my wife, leaning against the doorframe. She didn't speak and I didn't acknowledge her presence for fear she might ask what I was doing. After a moment, she walked away, heading downstairs to start breakfast and watch live news coverage of the latest global catastrophes.

I searched many hours of the recording before reaching what must have been Thursday's conference meeting. It began quietly, the same way Tuesday's meeting had begun. Twelve conferees entered the room and seated themselves, not speaking a single word. But, the moment the door closed, one lady spoke up.

"A man out there keeps looking at us."

She described a man with glasses in a plaid shirt, brown cardigan and navy Dockers — obviously me. Two others replied they knew who she meant, but hadn't noticed me noticing them.

"He's definitely got an eye on us," stated one of the other ladies.

"You've noticed, too?"

"Oh yea. When we went to leave Tuesday, he was, like, pretending to read the Sexual Harassment / Anti-discrimination / or *whatever* poster, but you could tell he was just standing there, listening and watching."

"He was probably checking you girls out," joked Paul Simon. "Working up the courage to ask one of you out on a date."

"Ya. Well, I hope that's all it is."

They were silent after that, each going about their individual business. Five minutes and 19 seconds later, the first lady, the one who noticed me, spoke again.

"What is it, you think, they're doing out there?"

"Who? What do you mean?"

"Those people."

Someone cleared his throat.

Another man spoke. "That's none of our business, Livia."

"You think? They probably know more about what's happening here than we do. If everything's going under, we'd be the last to hear. We're so out of the loop."

"Maybe that's why they're keeping an eye on us."

"Who's keeping an eye on us?"

"Them?"

There was a pause as if they were all silently staring out the conference door into the adjoining office space, or listening for sounds through the wall.

Finally, Pako broke the silence. "Let's not rock the boat," he said. "In my experience, the less you know, the better."

There was a harsh, guttural noise, clearly not in my headphones. I turned. It was my wife again. She had on her navy, wool overcoat and a black laptop bag over one shoulder.

I removed my headphones. "What's up?"

"I got a call. I need to go review a case and make a report."

"Was there an incident?"

"There's always an incident. I'll see you later, huh?" She stepped toward me and lightly touched my shoulder, before turning to leave. She asked nothing about what I was doing. Her thoughts were elsewhere. Work again.

The front door closed. The aluminium screen slammed back on its coil spring. I walked to the end of the hall and peered out from the sheer window curtains. There was a car waiting below, a large, black sedan. Exhaust poured from its tailpipe, diffusing into clouds of noxious air. As my wife lowered herself into the passenger seat, the driver gazed up. I stepped away from the window, but not before registering her face. The dark eyes. The widow's peak. The pencil thin brows. The spitting image of Elvira, one of the conferees at the Institute.

Of course, it couldn't actually be her. The same Elvira. That would mean they were all in cahoots — my wife, the conference group, the Institute, Skeye Lynx security. Such a nexus was highly unlikely. Right? But — but perhaps the high-unlikeliness was the very thing that made it likely. That's how things worked in the world today. The unexpected was the new expected. You had to keep on your toes, assume the thing coming is the very thing you're not expecting. The only truly irrational thing to expect is continued normalcy.

The engine started. Pebbles crunched beneath car tires as the sedan began to roll. I backed away from the curtains. The whirring engine and spewing gravel seemed amplified by the narrow hallway. I retreated into the spare bedroom and shut the door. Still, I could hear the high-pitched engine and the rattle of something loose beneath the hood. I pressed play, set the headphone over my ears, held them tightly in place.

Sliding window blinds. Humming AC. Clattering computer keys. Deep sighs. Stomach growls. Chiming phone apps. The sounds of the conference room filled my head once more. And yet they could not completely drown out the noise of the black sedan. No matter how loud I turned the volume, the black sedan's noise bled through — its popping gears, its gnarling carburettor, its squealing alternator and the sinister rive of gravel spewing from beneath its endlessly grinding and spinning tires.

Dictionary

There is nothing in the dictionary that quite helps me. There is nothing but words. Occasionally a picture. A simple line drawing. But mostly words. Definitions. Sample sentences. Pronunciation guides. Syntax. Why don't they put food in the dictionary? Doesn't have to be anything perishable. A little square of chocolate. Some dried fruit. A packet of instant coffee. Something to sit on, too, so you could settle in while flipping through its pages contemplating the inadequacy of dictionaries. Maybe something to listen to, also, like a soundtrack. Why hasn't anyone written a soundtrack for dictionaries? It would bring them to life. Fill them with suspense and drama. How difficult could that be? Add an earphone jack or bluetooth connection. *Duh*. Easy. There should be good lighting too. Hemingway wrote that a clean well-lighted place is a refuge from despair. Why not contain such light and space within a dictionary? There is nothing that says a dictionary must have size limitations or light restrictions.

Some say dictionaries are lonely places. Well, I say that. If you're like me, troubled by isolation and loneliness, you should have a dictionary that's inviting, where lots of people can gather. *Meet me at the dictionary at 7:30pm. Hurry before it closes.* Hell, make it a 24-hour dictionary. Always open. No cover. All ages. People can stop in anytime, day or night. Perfect for insomniacs. How great would that be?

Instead of a bunch of words sitting there, you'd have friends and families. Even complete strangers. You could walk up, introduce yourself. Say, *Hi, I'm Jeremy. What's your name?* And of course they would have a name, or could choose a name, because every dictionary worth half its salt includes many lists of names. You could talk about etymologies, expressions, usage — whatever, really. Or nothing at all! Why does a dictionary have to be about something? It doesn't. You could sit there in silence with this new person you've just met. Stare into each other's eyes. A finger pressed gently to lip. A silent communion. A kissless kiss. A meaning undefined, free from the claustrophobic burden of explanation.

The Recipe

The recipe called for flour, brown sugar and half-a-cup of butter. Add to that citrus rinds, currants and the stems of fresh berries. Mix in the husk of a coconut, the hairs of a wasp and the meat of a lamprey eel. Simmer with the smoke of mesquite, the heat of mating beetles, the dying breath of Karl Marx and the sweat of a pederast's left palm. While thickening, add the healing waters of Lourdes: one half ounce, blessed by no less than an Archbishop. In a separate bowl, place the shadow of a gull's wing, the whispers of a newborn calf, the failing bladder of an ex-Marine and the toupee of a former Communist apparatchik.

The recipe called for vandalised mausoleum cornices, the redemption of sin, the signatures of three authorized Volvo mechanics, the blue light of a glacier's reflection and the finely combed nose hairs of a Methodist minister. The recipe called for dangerous glances, for loose boulders, for momentary lapses in reason. The recipe called for mistaken identity, poorly worded questions and the loose fit of pre-washed gabardine. The recipe warned against autumn mist, insect bites and end-of-summer swimwear sales. The recipe advocated full body warmth, the secretion of breast milk and the fondling of amphibious mammals. The recipe also included plastic explosives, non-linear thinking, Armenian tapestry, the saliva of an on-duty border patrol guard, the grass over a pauper's grave and chipped porcelain from a pre-war Hummel figurine.

II.

The recipe imagined going on dates, slurping in the backseat of a Chevrolet, watching the sun rise over the Pacific, sautéing in the wet sand. The recipe wanted steady work, affordable rent and convenient public transportation. The recipe mastered Spanish and Italian, went for long strolls, spoke to friends about plans to travel, about great lands yet to be discovered, about its fear of dying and its early origins. The recipe relished the sight of moulting birds and blooming azaleas, savoured the smell of fresh bread and brisk morning air after a long night of rain. The recipe took in a movie now and then, bought frivolous gifts for friends and relatives, kept up a semi-fashionable wardrobe, discovered it looked really good in glass bowls. The recipe bit nails, chewed pens, broke glass, burned pans. The recipe drove too quick, frequently overdrew its checking account, ran up serious credit card debt. The recipe avoided paperwork, met friends for happy hour, stayed out too late. The recipe binged. The recipe fermented. The recipe rolled tobacco and flicked ashes beneath barstools. The recipe

quoted William Carlos Williams *The descent beckons /
as the ascent beckoned. / Memory is a kind / of accomplishment.* The recipe was a show off. The recipe was a
buffoon. The recipe was also remorseful and knew
when it had gone too far, making lavish apologies and
humble prostrations to the offended and repulsed. The
recipe was a complicated piece of work. The recipe met
promiscuous women. The recipe took them to dinner.
The recipe bought them drinks. The recipe lured them
home, making sloppy, reckless, tray-rattling sex. The
recipe discouraged substitute ingredients.

III.

The recipe became nervous, agitated, sentimental, stirred
up. The recipe was overwrought, tremulous, lacrimo-
nious. The recipe sought medical advice, doctors, psychi-
atrists, homeopaths, gastroenterologists. The recipe took
extracts and infusions. The recipe lamented it had not
known its origins better. The recipe forswore flavor en-
hancers. The recipe wanted posterity. The recipe joined a
compendium. The recipe shared. The recipe opened up to
strangers. The recipe meditated, coagulated, hydrated,
ululated before sunrise each morning. The recipe started
seeing someone much younger than itself. A beautiful
dish, well garnished, shy except while simmering upon
cast iron. The recipe fell in love, proposed. The recipe
produced progeny. The recipe doted over its creation.
The recipe swore off alcohol, beef, trans fats, processed
flour and vaping. The recipe was happier than it had
been in years.

But the recipe eventually developed sores, discol-

orations, flatulence and flees. Samples were taken, tests conducted. It was discovered the recipe had incurable bad aftertaste. The recipe wept. The recipe lamented. The recipe felt abandoned by its creator. The recipe became reclusive. The recipe hated itself, hated the world and its cruelty. The recipe didn't understand. The recipe had never asked for much, was not tasteless, was not ill conceived. The recipe burned everything, all notes and records, all cards and catalogues. The recipe took its family down the coast to a small enclave where they rented a place in the forest and grew vegetables and saw a good saucier twice daily who provided tarragon, sage, chilli and salt. The recipe began tasting better, but still contained deep-seated resentment. Eventually, the recipe had difficulty staying fully prepped. The recipe necessitated sinsemilla just to retain any sense of substance. The recipe went all day in a cannabinoid haze, feeling more peaceful than it had in months, but without any interest in being with others, dining out, or even simmering on low. The recipe hungered only for garden strolls, quiet naps, and coddling. The recipe was rapidly losing sustenance. The recipe's companion did its best to make things comfortable. The recipe realized it still felt love and was grateful. The recipe, on its final day, called its young progeny to its side, drew a difficult last breath and said, "I hope you're taking this all down."
IV.

When the recipe was gone, we tried to recall how much we knew. "It was hot," stated Kima, "but not Mexican hot. More like Indian hot." "I didn't think it was spicy," said Salali. "A bit smokey, maybe, if you know what I mean; not mesquite smokey, but more brown-coal smokey." "First time I made the recipe," began Clarisa, "was for my fiancé's parents. Gawd! That was a mistake. When Brock's father asked what was in it, he nearly spit out a mouthful. His mum loved it, though!" "Go figure," said Dawson, "People loved it or hated it." "I used to leave out certain parts," said Brian. "That's cheating," said Laman. "If you're not following the recipe precisely, you're not really making it." "I strongly disagree," said Paulo. "The recipe is a suggestion, a general idea. You should be able to play around with it. Improvise." "Maybe with a bad recipe." replied Laman, "but with a good recipe, everything matters. The choices are not arbitrary. Someone put a great deal of thought behind how everything works together." "That's too doctrinaire for my taste," said Steve. "I like to add a personal touch." "Then it becomes your own recipe," said Bertram. "Exactly," said Steve. "But," Bertram continued, "we're not, then, talking about the same thing." "What do you mean?" asked Steve. "We're trying to recall this particular recipe. Did we all have the same experience, taste the same thing? Or did we each experience something different?" "It was different each time for me," said Chyanne.

Kayah spoke out, "Jerry, you must remember the recipe."

"The recipe?" responded Jerry.

"Yes," said Kayah, "the recipe. The one we had. Do you remember?"

"Oh! The recipe," said Jerry, "The recipe changed everything. Absolutely everything!"

"Can you recite it or write it down for us?"

"Write what down?"

"The recipe, Jer'. Do you remember it?"

"Oh, the recipe! No. No, but..." Jerry appeared about to continue. The others waited. He paused, silently trying to recall the recipe, then resumed speaking. "I remember remembering the recipe." He wet his lips. "I remember thinking about the recipe. Just thinking about the recipe — any recipe — that's its own sort of hungry."

Out of the Blue

I was once lauded as some sort of hero, but I'm not really. Never was. Most people would have made the same choices. It's only nobody before me questioned the system. We simply accepted this state of affairs about the weather — it being a perfectly lawful, rather mundane phenomenon, whose complexity nevertheless vastly exceeds our ability to understand it. But that's hooey. If we can point out the causes of human misery and unhappiness — conditions determined by factors far more complex than mere weather — we can surely get at the root cause of intemperate rains and puckish winds.

Which is what I did. And it came as no small surprise how easy it was to manage. Regulating basic phenomena such as air temperature or cloud cover is no big deal, really. The solutions were lying right out in the open. I unhesitatingly took matters into my own hands — rigging climate, jiggering the atmosphere, arousing fresh winds and revitalising old pressure systems. Easy breezy.

My very first efforts focused on blue skies. That did

not go unnoticed. Clement weather is not commonplace in these parts. People looked up. Thought, *What the hell? A moderate 78°F. Iconic blue skies. Billowy white clouds. Warm, caressing rays of light. Gentle zephyr winds…How did this happen?*

Word got out I was responsible. I must say I enjoyed the attention. "Nice job with the weather," people would say. "Keep up the good work."

Despite a large outpour of support, there remained some who would not deign acknowledge my accomplishment. (You know who you are.) They sought to undermine my work by pointing out the illegality of what I was doing, making climate change without proper authorization — no permits, no professional qualifications, accreditation or licensing. But what did any of that matter? Let the results speak for themselves.

So I thought.

But the government thought otherwise. One day officials from the Council of Environmental Quality (CEQ) arrived at my door. Dark, worsted wool suits, bleached hair and refractive, orange sunglass lenses. They questioned me for hours. Police detectives followed. I was escorted to my local precinct. Charges filed. News media everywhere.

The case became an imbroglio for the feds and their panel of "expert" witnesses. Leading up to the trial, the general public had begun to question why, for so long, we had had such crummy, and sometimes catastrophic, weather if there are so-called *experts* running the show. And how could they, the government, prosecute someone like me for simply, effectively and selflessly improving weather conditions for one and all?

The law is the law, said government prosecutors. Judge Maryanne J. Gilliard agreed. In the end I was convicted, but only required to pay a small fine. The fine and attorney fees were easily covered by a legal defence fund established during my incarceration after my situation went viral on social media.

My defence team believed my constitutional rights had been violated and were willing to appeal the decision. Until the appeal was heard (who knew how long that would take?), I was told to mind my own business, lay low, keep my filthy paws off the cloud cover.

This galled me. I had worked hard for better weather. And I'd only just begun showing how great weather could truly be when properly managed. I could not let my super-stratospheric good deeds go to waste. So, covertly, I continued my work, refining skills and finessing results — all the while ensuring these barometric changes could not be traced back to me.

Weather improved beyond people's wildest dreams. And the more weather I created, the more aware I became of subtle nuances in atmosphere I hadn't noted before. There are ways of milking intensity out of a ruddy sunset by nimbly joining thin, undulating cirrus clouds to plush cirrostratus vapours. I learned how to mix spectral hues and create shimmering tones for dramatic contrast. Sky was theatre. Weather, a play I staged. Various cloud forms could be hung like curtains, lighting gels and scrim. Deep, endless fog placed as a backdrop could accentuate foreground luminosity. The more I experimented, the further potential I discovered for creative expression.

I tested some colorful aurora lights. Mostly to see if I could pull them off. I was pleasantly surprised with the results. From there I tried trickier stuff, like a fogbow (a rainbow stuffed inside a roll of fog). I had some complaints about the carbon emissions used to create this. But the bow itself — its striking fringe of red, ochre and aquatic blue — was well worth the quibble and fuss.

I proceeded cautiously, trying to stick to what I believed were more innocuous formations, such as Dust Devils. (They're fun to whip up and kids love chasing them.) My Altocumulus Undulatuse became popular amongst many evening strollers for its enchanting, green iridescence. Yet even this mild weather condition had its detractors, those who complained the Altocumuli Undulatuses of their youths were brighter, greener and far more joyful.

No weather pleases everyone. And nostalgia is a curse.

I gave up trying to serenely satisfy. I thought people should be provoked into amazement and wonder. So I created tall, glorious funnel clouds. As long as they remain airborne, there's no real danger. But, of course, not everyone was thrilled by my funnel-cloud spectacular. Some claimed to have been traumatized. Some cancelled important meetings. Anxious cows wouldn't milk. Cabbies couldn't cab. Flights were grounded. And the feeble hearted developed arrhythmia.

A similar, negative response was elicited by my Beaver's Tail (a sort of low inflow of cloud cover that fans out like a bushy beaver tail). People complained it looked like a nuclear explosion.

Friends began to warn I was taking things too far, drawing too much attention to the weather. Authorities had begun to note the unconventional climate patterns. Suspicions were raised among the weather bureau and CEQ. Windowless vans parked outside my home. Dark figures trailed me through streets and alleys. *Play it safe*, I was told. *Just stick to blue skies. Nothing but blue skies. You're good at those. Don't overreach.*

I felt cornered by the cretinous demands of the general public and the vigilant eye of the authoritarian state. So I relented. If blue skies were what they wanted, then blue skies were what they'd get. I'd shove blue skies down their philistine throats. Endless blue upon blue.

They couldn't get enough. *Keep it coming*, they said. *This is what we crave*, they said. Yet they were more miserable than ever. They had no understanding why. They thought more blue skies was the solution, the fix to all their troubles and woes. *Can it get any bluer than this?* they queried. *Give us all the blue you got, buddy.*

Occurrences of teenage wilding began to escalate. The warm night air elicited marauding packs of scantily clad youth. They roamed the streets, restless, agitated. They gathered in moonlit fields to imbibe fermented juice, smoke weed, light bonfires, dance themselves into a rabid frenzy and engage in risky sex and other deviant behavior. Fights broke out for the most trivial reasons. Graffiti and vandalism proliferated. Vacant buildings were set ablaze. Plumes of black smoke rose, smudging the bejewelled black velvet of my perfect night skies.

What people want and what they need are two different things. Prosaic blue skies and anodyne, cotton ball clouds only lure people into complacency. Obsequious weather conditions eradicate all drive and ambition, seducing us into apathy and dullness. Lack of environmental stimulation prevents true progress. They couldn't see it from their perspective, but I could. Only those who create truly know the lay of the land.

To hell with playing it safe, I thought. These people don't understand what's best for them. They need to be inspired by weather. To be in awe. Kept alert. Days must be differentiated, the passage of time made manifest by celestial notation. The variability of deluges, draught, shifting airstreams, drifting cloud formations, heaving tides — these patterns must all be employed, like narratives, to guide people forward in time.

I got back to work. I assembled a dramaturgy of effects. I began to create new, inspiring weather patterns once more. I tested ideas. I revived old classics. I took notes, made observations. A tenebrous night storm made the morning spectral rays all the more glorious to behold. A thorough chinook expelled stagnant vapours, pollens, spores, bacteria, fumes, mites, fleas and more.

Ya. Things got knocked around. Doors slammed. Windows broke. Grannies got knocked on their arses. Umbrellas snapped. Old barns toppled. But there is no true growth without change. And no true change without loss. The old leaves and branches must fall. Fruits and flowers must scatter amidst winds. Carcasses must decompose beneath torrents. Weather must set the stage for new forms of life to be rendered active and available.

Inspiration took hold. I tried my hand at bigger things, like anvil crawlers — those sparkly ribbons of light that creep beneath flat-bottomed clouds. I perfected those suckers for months. Harmless, I assure you. The few pillars of lighting that burst down from the crawlers were a different matter. Completely unintentional. An unpleasant side effect. Yes, one did completely destroy the Lutheran church on Regent Street. And another took the life of Gerald Bentley — who was, by the way, already quite old at the time. But it was, in no way, my intention to spark cloud-to-ground lightning. And I pretty much fixed that problem so it would never happen again. So, really, I didn't understand why all the scorn and reprobation surrounding these somewhat unfortunate events.

The massive public protest against me and my work was incited by a few, grandiloquent TV personalities. Particularly, one former news weatherman, a pseudo scientist with an online meteorology degree. Wes Stapleton had his own call-in show on WLGN. He implicated me in Gerald Bentley's death. Accused me of the foul weather. Claimed I had messianic delusions of grandeur, that I was some crazed psycho. He mocked my protective foil head gear. Defamation. Jealousy. Grandstanding. C'mon. This guy is a former local news forecaster. A TV "weatherman." Why would anyone listen to him?

But they did. And they organized. They protested out my window. They gathered day and night, waving banners and cardboard signs. GIVE US BACK OUR BLUE SKIES. HANDS OFF THE JET STREAM. MIND YOUR OWN METEOROLOGY.

FREE THE TRADE WINDS. NO MORE GAILS. END THE HAVOC NOW!

CEQ authorities showed up at my door once again asking questions. They had search warrants, canines, cameras and trace detection swabs. They ransacked the place, pulled up linoleum, unstuffed seat cushions, peeled off shelf liners. Their dogs sniffed at my upholstery and between my linens. They carted off all my personal electronics, my entire collection of crystals and a half dozen unsent, extremely-personal letters in foil-pressed stationery. They bagged, zip-tied and labeled anything they thought could be used against me.

I'm no idiot. I know how to cover my trail. They could make no connection between me and anything to do with the weather. No legitimate connection, that is. But this is how the world works: anyone in power who is out to get you *will* get you. Operate outside the system and they will eventually come down on you. Hard. And they did.

I don't regret anything, though. I could have played it safe, given them what they wanted. Blue sky after boring, *la dee da* blue sky. But fudge that. I was doing great work, making skies beyond the imaginable. Giving people real experiences. Letting them sense nature's magnificent might, its brutal, incalculable power. This is what puts our lives in context with our vast universe. A universe in which we are just motes adrift upon curlicue wisps of fractal energy waves. It amazes me that people fail to see this, that they are so willing to opt for the routine and common when nature offers such great beauty and spectacle.

I have been in detention now for some forty days while awaiting trial. For forty days and nights the weather has gone pell-mell to hell as state bureaucracy struggles to reach consensus over re-establishing weather control — all the while mangling the magnificent systems I'd painstakingly put in place.

My detractors hold me responsible for the current weather debacle. The propaganda employed against me is astounding. Mainstream media portrays me as a literal lunatic, an obsessive control freak living in a delusional state of psychosis after suffering a long series of romantic rejections, career failures and restraining orders. But they don't know me. What do those clods understand about true devotion? Or love? Real love. Unbridled longing. Tempestuous desire. Passion as hot and tropical as a Westerly Wind.

Oh Sharla June! If you'd only remained in town long enough to see what I could accomplish! To see those anvil crawlers and multi-hued borealises. To succumb to my fog bow and beaver's tail. To realize I was a true artist after all. If you had only gazed but once upon the splendour of my phosphorescent updrafts and grand auroras! Your love would yet be mine!

Little Beast

When I got back, I was dying to pee. Nearly wet my pants when switching on the light. Startled by something moving out the corner of my eye. A dull thump. In the bath. Something dark against white enamel. A clump of hair. Arms and legs jiggling from a ball of fur. Trying desperately to claw its way out. Getting nowhere.

Wire clothes hanger in hand, I leaned over the tub. It scrambled away. Then turned toward me. It seemed like some strange amalgamate of monkey, rat and Sharpei pup. Not much bigger than my fist. It was the eyes, though. Those eyes. The eyes of a human infant. Big and moist and empty-headed.

I'd never seen a beast close up. You see them in movies and documentaries, not everyday life. I worried how it got into my place. Or, worse, where its mother was. I reached for a towel. A frayed blue towel I didn't mind ruining. I could easily smother it, toss it into an alley dumpster. Do it quick, I thought. Before it gets away.

As I loomed over the little beast, prepared to crush

its skull, our eyes met and — *for fuck's sake* — it appeared so human. So horribly human.

Its eyes watched me, fearful and imploring. Pull it together, I told myself. You're attributing human emotions to a beast. If it's thinking anything, it's about escape or killing. Flight or fight. But for me to kill, I worried — did that make me no better than a beast?

I trapped the beast beneath a plastic wash bucket. Held the bucket in place with a box of old vinyl LPs. From the basement storage, I retrieved a pet cargo crate that belonged to previous tenants. I brushed off the dust and spider webs, and caged the beast inside.

Emily didn't want to sleep in the same room with the beast. She made me keep it locked in the laundry room while we were in bed. When we had sex I, too, heard its long black nails scraping against the sides of its crate.

The beast grew bigger. They grow faster than oxtail. It became the size of an adult raccoon. I kept it on harness and leash. Never allowed it to leave the house. What would the neighbors say?

Emily said, "If you don't kill the damn thing, I will."

"Go ahead then," I said. And meant it. It would be a weight off my shoulders.

Emily stood above the beast, shovel in hand, ready to strike. It sat there, silently watching her, waiting. She hesitated. Then lowered the shovel. She couldn't do it, either.

"Oh fuck," she said. "Keep it. I just don't ever want it in the same room with me when I'm over."

I didn't live in that house for long. Eventually, I had

enough well-paying clients to afford a nicer place outside town, surrounded by meadows and a grove of chestnuts. Emily was living full time with me by then, despite her aversion to the beast. I first kept it chained in the basement. But when it made too much noise at night — clanging its irons and yowling — I installed a steel-enforced, wooden shed in the backyard and kept the beast locked inside it.

I had dreams about the beast. I dreamt about killing it. Sometimes by poison. Sometimes with a blow to the head. Sometimes I let it starve to death. In sleep, I felt no remorse. But I would awake feeling disgust. Who am I? Who am I, really?

I enjoyed working at home. But my work required occasional travel. That left Emily alone with the beast. She cared for it like yard work, a chore she neither hated nor enjoyed. Just part of her routine. At least that's what she led me to believe.

One day I returned home from a business trip and found the door to the shed open. My heart beat so fiercely I thought it might burst apart. Had it escaped? Then I saw inside the shed. Emily splattered in mud. Half naked. The beast in full straddle. Working his little beastly parts between her spread thighs. Emily moaning so loud, she could not hear me scream her name.

Things were different after that. Not in the way I would have expected. Emily and I reached an understanding. We agreed to get rid of the beast. We found a buyer online. Illegally, of course. There is no country in which such transactions are legal. Except maybe Serbia. We had to take precautions. We used an encryption key from a non-centralized web server and a third-party verification code to ensure we were dealing with an actual buyer and not some government agency or bestial rights organization trying to entrap us.

The buyer communicated responses through anonymous message boards. His English was rudimentary. There was confusion about payment at first. But that got sorted. Five days later, he arrived at our place. A black Mercedes sedan. Tinted windows. Towing a blue and white EZ Haul trailer. Handed us cash. Drove the beast away. No paperwork. No questions asked.

A year or so passed. Emily was sick. Said something was wrong with her. Doctor said she was pregnant. We had not planned on a child. But weren't entirely against it. We began preparing for a family. Baby clothes. Second-hand crib. Parenting magazines. I painted flying horses, clouds and rainbows on one wall of the spare bedroom. We picked out a name. Judy, if it's a girl. Jason, if it's a boy.

Emily had bad dreams. She feared something was not right with the baby. "That's normal," I said. "Those kinds of dreams are typical for pregnant women." I didn't know if that was true. I assumed it was. I wanted to ease her mind. I kept my own fears about the child to myself.

Emily turned out to be right. I delivered the baby. Finished delivering it, actually. The midwife fainted midway through birth. That dark bundle of wet hair with tiny claws was no baby. Not any sort of human baby. I took the blade, severed the umbilical cord and held the knife over it. My hands shook.

Emily whispered, "No." I dropped the knife. I drew

open the window. I threw the beast far into the tall weeds below.

That same evening, I drove to The Saloon on Old 92. A cab driver next to me at the bar kept saying, "You ain't gotta go home. You ain't gotta go home. You gotta be a man, you know? Like really a man." I didn't know what the fuck he was getting at.

The bartender asked me, "If you could be anyone in the world, who would you be?"

The cabbie slapped a 20 dollar bill on the bar counter and laughed.

I took my beer to a table beside the popcorn machine. It made the bar smell like the lobby of an old cinema. Near me sat a man wearing large glasses with thick yellow lenses. He held a red, cloth-bound book close to his face. Trying to read within the dim barroom light.

Some old perv, I thought. Who else reads in a bar? The moment I thought this, the man looked up. I averted my eyes. Took a deep swig of beer.

"Oh?"

I pretended not to hear him.

He continued, "Think what you like."

"Excuse me?"

"I was reading something interesting. *Very* interesting."

"Hmmm," I said.

"Ancient Sumerian law had murderers executed and buried with their victims. That way the victim can revenge himself in the next life. Or the life after. Or the life after that if he kept failing to do so. Interesting now, isn't it?"

"If you're into that Sumerian stuff. Personally, I prefer a good Pilsner."

"It's all a big circle, see?" He held open the book. Pointed to a diagram. I glanced, then turned away. I drank my beer and returned the empty glass to the bar. This town is full of old kooks like that.

On the way home, I took backroads. Didn't want to risk being pulled over. The road was narrow. Someone came at me with high-beams. I couldn't see. I swerved. My head hit the steering wheel. I remember Ricky Martin singing "Livin' La Vida Loca" on the radio. I remember drops of water on the windshield. Beads catching and reflecting red tail lights. I remember the taste of metal in my mouth. Not sure how long I sat there. I waited for my nerves to calm. Then made my way back home.

When I got back, I was dying to pee. Nearly wet my pants when switching on the light. Startled by something moving out the corner of my eye. A dull thump. In the bath. Something dark against white enamel. A clump of hair. Arms and legs jiggling from a ball of fur. Trying desperately to claw its way out. Getting nowhere.

Wire clothes hanger in hand, I leaned over the tub. It scrambled away. Then turned toward me. It seemed like some strange amalgamate of monkey, rat and Sharpei pup. Not much bigger than my fist. It was the eyes, though. Those eyes. The eyes of a human infant. Big and moist and empty-headed.

I worried how it got into my place. Or, worse, where its mother was.

Meet Our Contributors

Hanson Scott Spear is probably best known for his trilogy, *The Powder Mountain Dairy*, one of the most extensive literary works ever produced about Wisconsin's cheese industry, beginning with the early Swiss homesteads and encompassing its 20th-century mass marketing and diversification into hotels, entertainment and casinos. His first published novel, *Garbo, Meine Liebe*, about an obsessive transgender serial killer, was awarded the Pembroke Prize for Best First Fiction and the Helen Geissbuhler Award for Young Writers. His other novels include *Sleeping With Satan, Kiosk Bordello, Here Comes the Warm, Wet Wind*, and *Pirate! Debutante! Zombie!* (a multimedia novel sold with DVD, 3-D glasses and recipe cards). He is the author of two collections of critical essays, "Hey, Chaucer!" and "The Wasteland Wasn't and Other Essays." His children's book, created with illustrations by performance artist Diva Claire A'day, titled *Blood Sacrifice*, will be published next year by Rhubarb Press. He is the author of numerous short stories, including "The Trouble with Colored People," "Lincoln's

Handbag," "Kitty's Bahama Holiday," and "Dimples" — all of which have widely appeared in anthologies, journals and on his own highly acclaimed website, SuccessfulWriter.com.

One of the most prolific writers in modern history, **Constance Beckford** has been a major force in the development of popular women's literature. Her stunning debut novel, *Roger is a Misogynistic A-Hole* broke new ground in publishing history. As editor of the monthly periodical "Tampon Explosion," Beckford ushered in a new wave of "angry chick lit" and brought attention to many new voices in the world of Emasculatory Womyn's Writing. Her series of "Dumb Fucker" novels (titled *Unwise Men* in their Vantage Press paperback editions), redefined the Romance novel and began a late 1980s publishing trend in which many women authors explored ways to alienate male readers while still provoking their prurient interest. Her latest novel, *Gonorrhea: A Love Story* deals with the Cuban Missile Crisis and female genital mutilation in Ontario.

Less Greenwald is widely regarded as one of the most exciting writers of the 1890s. His stories have appeared in The Munsey Journal, Josiah Strong's Strange Tales, Cavalcade of Stories and Puppin Magazine. His books include *Ahmed's Magic Buggy, Gay Horizons, A Brief Treatise Upon the Mating Rhino* and *Thy Pilgrim's Honour*. In addition to his fiction, Greenwald has also written the libretto for the musicals *Young Soldier, My*

Heart Beats for Thee and *Dr. Shriver's Magical Pink Potion*. His incomplete, posthumously published novel *Armageddon 'Round the Bend* was the recipient of the Philibin Hayes Award for Morally Upstanding Literature.

Born in Ibadan, Nigeria, **Thomas Winterbottom** now lives in North Adams, Massachusetts where he is Professor of Journalism and Public Relations at Massachusetts College of Liberal Arts. Winterbottom sold his first story, "Afrikers Red Bananas" to Transglobal Vibrations in 1975 and has produced over 840 stories since, many having been anthologized in his own compendium of International Literature, *Tribal Beat Happening*. He was award the Consumer Satisfaction Award for his story "Whitey's Pernicious Lies." He resides with his wife Jennifer and their two English Setters, Dido and Aeneas.

Carey Malcolm is a novelist, short-story writer, and journalist. His distinctive writing style is characterized by economy and understatement, and has had a significant influence on the development of twentieth century fiction. Malcolm became a member of a group of expatriate Americans in Paris, which he described in his first important work, *The Sun Also Rises*. Equally successful was his novel *A Farewell to Arms*, the study of an American ambulance officer's disillusionment in war and his role as a deserter. Malcolm, nicknamed "Papa," used his experiences as a reporter during the Spanish

Civil War as background for his most ambitious novel, *For Whom the Bell Tolls*. Among his later works, the most outstanding is the short novel, *The Old Man and the Sea*, the story of an ageing fisherman's journey, his long and lonely struggle with a fish and the sea, and his victory in defeat. In his later years, Malcolm suffered from writer's block, acute depression and allegations of plagiarism.

THE WEATHER IN FRITZ BEMELMANS PARK by Holly Tavel
ISBN 978-0-9571213-9-3. Paperback. 152pp. November 2015.
"Tavel's worlds are magically palpable, rendered in precise detail and a moody palette just beyond reach of reality. [...] Tavel's voice is both comic and elegiac, with a deep sadness underlining the absurdity."
Angela Woodward

MOURNING by Richard Makin
ISBN 978-0-9931955-2-5. Paperback. 254pp. May 2015.
"This is prose you must learn to experience before you begin to interpret... the pages in their beautiful and delirious abstraction are ordered poetry." Iain Sinclair

H by Philippe Sollers;
translated by Veronika Stankovianska & David Vichnar
ISBN 978-0-9931955-0-1. Paperback. 172pp. May 2015.
"The literary scholars of Prague have set the trend for literary publishing in the translation of *H,* a key work of the French avant garde novel which exemplifies philosophical and Abstract Expressionist esthetic theories from the experimental decade of the 70s." David Detrich

DOCTOR BENJAMIN FRANKLIN'S DREAM AMERICA
by Damien Lincoln Ober
ISBN 978-0-9571213-8-6. Paperback. 279pp. October 2014.
"Ober's mix of heady ideas and gorgeous prose make this a uniquely compelling debut. *DBFDA* is nothing less than an alternate history of the birth of the United States that hints at our coming demise."
Jim Ruland

CAIRO by Louis Armand
ISBN 978-0-9571213-7-9. Paperback. 366pp. January 2014.
"A genre defying anti-novel... Like communism it is the movement of vast majorities unfettered by a state!" Stewart Home

ONLY FOOLS DIE OF HEARTBREAK by Thor Garcia
ISBN 978-0-9571213-4-8. Paperback. 340pp. April 2013.
"A book that, if published in the 19th century, would have given Charles Darwin's *Origin of Species* and Mark Twain's *Huckleberry Finn* a run for their money as the most controversial and banned book in the nation." *Necessary Fiction*

LOUIS XXX by Georges Bataille; translated by Stuart Kendall
ISBN 978-0-9571213-5-5. Paperback. 142pp. April 2013.
"An obscure work in the history of transgressive literature has, for
the first time, been given definitive and due recognition." Matt Pincus

CANICULE by Louis Armand
ISBN 978-0-9571213-3-1. Paperback. 222pp. April 2013.
"[...] a Ballardian critique of modernity, where the beach is a wasteland and the balconied hotel rooms are ruins, and the people who go
about amongst them are dazed and shell-shocked survivors who do
not yet know that everything around them has been destroyed."
Bayard Godsave

THE NEWS CLOWN by Thor Garcia
ISBN 978-0-9571213-2-4. Paperback. 477pp. April 2012.
"A tapestry of a post-apocalyptic society whose debt-bound, clueless
denizens are so anaesthetized from noise, shopping and drugs, prescription or otherwise, that they are unaware the calamity they fear
as bogyman has already overtaken them." Jim Chaffee

BREAKFAST AT MIDNIGHT by Louis Armand
ISBN 978-0-9571213-0-0. Paperback.164pp. April 2012.
"A real delight, the kind of book that both embraces and breathes life
into the standard tropes associated with the hard-boiled genre [...] a
twisted, brilliantly savage acid noir." Benjamin Woodard

THE BRAIN HARVEST by Ken Nash
ISBN 978-0-9571213-1-7. Paperback. 159pp. April 2012.
"Nash is a storyteller in the most prime of forms, and years from
now, with this collection far, far away, I won't need the characters
and their situations as much as I'll need what I'll actually have, which
is the residuals." *Necessary Fiction*

CLAIR OBSCUR by Louis Armand
ISBN 978-80-260-0112-6. Paperback. 288pp. October 2011.
"This is a poet's novel, when it is not a filmmaker's or a painter's, and
should be enjoyed as a multimedia, multilinguistic experience."
Erik Martiny, *The Iowa Review*

www.ingramcontent.com/pod-product-compliance
Lightning Source LLC
Chambersburg PA
CBHW061026120726
47910CB00006B/2121